A Struggle of Ego
(Tom's Story)

Living Beyond Life

DEDICATION

This book is dedicated to Living Beyond Life and those who are free enough to do so.

As always, I must mention my editor, Karen, who has been there since the beginning and continues to do more for me and my books than anyone else. I would never get anything published without you.

CONTENTS

Author's Note

AUTHOR'S NOTE

Thank you for joining me in yet another search for the truth. This is my attempt at showing some of the pitfalls of hearing the ego over the deeper self. Ego is a tricky and cruel mistress who will often lead us astray. Those who think they have conquered it are the most susceptible to its wily nature. The goal of life, living beyond life, is the overall message of every book I have written thus far. Ego is a major part of life and it is my pleasure to offer this account of ego in action. The book is written in a way that may be too far along for some people to follow. I ask you to bear with it, and hope that you can learn from Tom's mistakes and his awareness.

Chapter 1
Life on the Run

There are a few things to know before I begin the story of what happened on that faithful day, when Tom was walking to the grocery store. No. Never mind. It won't make any sense, even if I did a good job of explaining it, so let's just get started. Suffice it to say that this ordinary world is not quite so ordinary for people like Tom. Everything is at his disposal, or that of his imagination (if you have a hard time understanding that these things are possible to those who are free). Tom was feeling casual as he flew through the air in his Volkswagen, on the way to the grocery store.

Those who could see through the thin shroud that covers our eyes from true existence, were laughing or shaking their heads because he wasn't following the rules. The rest of mankind watched him driving down the road as anyone normally would, with their eyes clouded to reality. Tom's car usually landed safely, but sometimes would explode into millions of pieces as he stood by and watched from afar wondering if he would be able to take out an insurance claim. As quickly as the car was destroyed, he would blink and see it sitting back in the parking space, where everyone else had seen it carefully pull in.

Sometimes Tom would create people who could see and react to it, so that life was like a movie, and a bit more entertaining for him. He had long ago accepted the failure and defeat of trying to accomplish anything on this Earth. People, things, events, and everything else was just so boring to him. Especially since he, quite literally, controlled the universe. Tom strode confidently toward the doors of the store, even though he was completely naked. Nobody could see that he wasn't wearing any clothes, which he quite enjoyed, feeling like it were a comedic movie, where everybody else was in on the joke too.

A bee flew around him for a few moments, causing Tom to swing his foot at it, a weird thing you know, when you control everything your mind still falls back on old habits. Fight or flight instinct still kicks in for a moment before he remembers that he is in charge of it. There is a brief flash of a bee sting and the pain that is related to it, though Tom would never have to worry about such things, it was still part of his past programming. The bee was gone. Tom's clothes had miraculously reappeared on his body at the sight of the bee. Not only being stung in general, but the idea of where it might happen, had frightened his programming into bringing back the protective clothing. Tom was free as we know it, yet he still had no freedom from himself. A self that he had already acknowledged was never him in the first place, but rather a collection of thoughts, ideas, and beliefs that were programmed into him by everyone in his surrounding environment as he grew up. The truth is, he was growing down.

Tom started life as someone with infinite potential to be anything and do anything. As per usual, society tried to limit it for him when he was young, through social conditioning. The problem he faced was that without ever having been programmed by these people, he would have no way of interacting with this world. Language and the way people exist here, was a necessary curse that would have to be accepted if one were to live on this planet productively. Not just productivity, it came down to the very simplest of actions. To the very words of language that sometimes plagued him as thoughts, yet meant so much for interaction. Tom would not be able to communicate with the world or even himself if he didn't play along.

Just to know and understand was not enough. Truth, as true as it ever could be, would not hold the necessary devices required to make small-talk with other people, or to pontificate existence with them. That was such a small thing to Tom, even though the idea of questioning reality is so great to the common man. His priorities of what mattered in life were a bit different. Tom had been spending his time mostly at home reading and learning about things that people thought were real. He knew it was all just a show. Every bit of knowledge these people claimed to have, was a laugh, but it was still fun to play the game and to see where it could lead. He often created people and played games with them, as we are about to see, but no matter how many people he kept around, he always felt alone in the world. Whether he created them or not, he couldn't help but control them in some fashion, or wonder if his subconscious programming was taking effect. Who was really in control?

Did it count as *his* decision when his subconscious forced itself upon them? What if that person hadn't wanted to smile at Tom? Did they have free-will in the first place, regardless of Tom and his subconscious? How could he know the reasoning behind anything and what was the difference between Tom making people smile at him and their original programming doing the same? It was very rarely their unique self. If it was their programming, it wasn't *really* their decision anyway, even if it seemed like it was. How could they have a choice if the life lessons they act on are already determined? Tom wished others could understand and let go of their programming. Their idea of self. He believed that people don't have to be a summation of their actions, but contrary that they choose to be, and with little resistance at that.

Some will argue that it is our choice to accept the programming, but remember the child who disobeys the programming and ends up with a spanking. He is sure to do the right thing next time. Whose idea of right is it? It becomes his even if it wasn't. That is, the choice that will not lead to the spanking becomes programmed as what is right. Is choosing to do something because of fear of punishment any worse than doing it just because Tom wanted them to? They were still a slave to someone, usually a parent or institution that programmed them before they ever crossed paths with Tom. The answer was situational to most people, but the fact is that most people never had an opportunity to even think about it, yet alone have an opinion on whether or not what he was doing was right, acceptable, or moral. Most of the time they aren't even told why afterward. They are punished with no real explanation, then they do the same to others when they are in charge. Just like the experiment where monkeys are punished for going near a banana. When a new monkey enters, the others will stop him if he tries to go near the banana, because of what happened to them.

Whatever people are worried about when they think about their rights being violated, it was already happening. We give the illusion of choice example, the child sees the options as twofold: obey or be punished. He thinks of those two options and picks the lesser of the two evils, thinking that by having two choices it was his decision, when any sane person as an adult would simply leave the situation and not indulge the parents. The same is happening with political elections, we are given the choice of two and act like we are making a decision. People choose because they hate one alternative a little less than the other, not because they want either one. It is a simple mind trick used by salesmen for hundreds of years. It is called the 'illusion of choice.' Thinking about this kind of thing tended to disturb his peacefulness, so Tom focused the next distraction as an easy way out.

He was always confused as to why this chapter was called 'Life on the Run,' when no one was really running in a literal sense. There was nothing to run from and nowhere in which to run. Where was there to go? Why was Tom even bothering to do anything at this point, when he could cease to exist at any moment and have nothing left to consider? Was that really a possibility? Disappearing. Was it just another attachment? An attachment to death in place of one clinging to life? Tom didn't really care either way. As far as he was concerned, it was the only thing to do. Whatever exists in the present moment is all there is. One thing is for sure, Tom was not running from the store, in fact, he had already walked through the sliding doors.

Tom didn't need anything from the store. He didn't *need* anything in general, really. He had the entire universe at his fingertips, but the other option was to sit there and do nothing like real saints do in India. That sounded boring to Tom. He did it anyway sometimes, and was never one of those people who said they couldn't meditate without having tried it, but it didn't particularly appeal to him most of the time. It didn't not appeal to him either, that was the predicament. He did his best to have no attachments. Everything was always fine. He would do what he was doing, just because he was doing it, and nothing happened either way, as far as he was concerned.

Tom played many roles, and had lost his enthusiasm for most of them. He noticed that he was drifting through the air, a few feet off the ground. This happened to him often when he was too busy letting his mind think, instead of paying attention to the present moment. As far ahead as he may have been in evolution, the mind kept talking over him, thinking about what it wanted to think about; trying to entertain him, protect him, control him, or simply occupy the time. That is one of the only times Tom would really be upset with himself, if there were such a thing (it was more likely still ego distracting him further), that is to say, he was bothered when his mind would get the upper-hand and talk about all of these things to him, causing him to miss what was going on right in front of him. He was upset when he got involved with it, instead of letting the thoughts go by.

He wasn't sure if there really was that much more going on in front of him, but it still felt like someone else was in control in those moments. Like blacking out then waking up. That was the feeling he got when he woke back up from whatever distraction the mind brought. How does one ever really know when control has been taken away? It is when one gives up the idea of control that he is free to do anything. Let go of want, need, attachment, then whatever happens is real, and there is no interpretation or suffering from it. Most of the time Tom would normally shrug it off, but this time he found himself falling to the floor on his back, looking at the boring fluorescent lights on the ceiling of the store that most people never notice. Even the light around us needs not have a source, if it is working properly. The moment it goes out, everyone notices there are greater forces around them keeping the place visible to our limited eyes. Nobody, while watching TV, would know the walls were missing if they didn't feel a draft. Likewise, nobody misses the sun until the day it doesn't rise.

Chapter 2
Sam

It was at that point a girl's face appeared upside down above his. "What are you doing down there?" she asked him.

"Existing. I was floating," John replied. Was this his mind trying to distract him? Was that thought?

"Well, you didn't do a very good job of it, if you find yourself down on the ground, huh?"

"Mind distracted me. I lost focus."

"I see. Does that happen often?"

"It does to all of us. Some people are just more aware than others of who is speaking in their head."

"Why were you floating?"

"No reason. It was just something to do in the moment, just like lying here looking at the ceiling, or talking to you."

"That was my reasoning as well, you know."

"Really?"

"That and I just had to ask that silly man why he was lying on the floor," she replied.

"I suppose I should get up then."

"I suppose you should."

"Do you want to see me float?"

"Not particularly. It isn't of great interest to me."

Tom started to levitate, about half a foot off the ground.

"I said I didn't care," said the girl, "it's not that impressive really, just another parlor trick. You probably use it to pick up women."

"Let's see you do it then. You really aren't impressed? I have seen people go crazy over less," Tom said, feeling indignant.

"They must have really wanted it then. I don't particularly have any interest."

Tom was having a hard time trying to understand this. Was it possible that his mind had found another way to trick him by bringing this girl here? People usually catered to his whims if his mind had it's say, not caused conflict. The mind abhors conflict. It doesn't know how to react. That is why we are present for a moment after a loud noise shocks us.

"What would impress you?" Tom asked.

"I was impressed by you lying there, actually, assuming you weren't crazy or dying."

"Do you think I am?"

"Dying? We're all dying at some pace. As for crazy, I haven't decided yet."

"I see. What's so special about lying here?"

"Nobody in their right mind would do such a thing, would they? I thought it was neat that you broke down the socially dictated barrier that keeps adults off the floors."

"Well said."

"I'm Sam," said the girl, extending her hand toward him.

"I didn't know that," Tom replied.

"Of course you didn't, how would you have known."

"I usually do know... everything. Anything. I mean, it's not me knowing it, just some connection with everything that allows me to know all truths," Tom said, starting to really wonder what was happening. Could his mind be so elaborate?

"That's neat."

8

"You don't believe me," Tom said.

"Well you did get that one right."

"That was just being perceptive."

"Does it matter if I believe you?" Sam asked.

"Normally I could tell you, but I honestly haven't figured it out yet. I usually have no doubts. I don't know what to make of it."

"Are you going to tell me your name?"

"I am Tom, the Master of all things," said Tom.

"Can I just call you Tom? If not, it's going to be T-MOAT."

"Yes, the rest is ego, I just made it up in the moment."

"That's less surprising than you'd think."

"You really want to talk to me?" Tom asked.

"I'm still here, aren't I?"

"It's just... I don't think I've had a real conversation with anyone in quite a long time... it's always been my own creation. This could be something I did subconsciously."

"Pfffft, it's not all about you. I just thought you seemed like an interesting person so I came over and asked what you were doing. Don't make me regret it."

Tom's mind was not computing what was happening. He was trying to understand it, but in order to do this he had to use his mind and the language of it. He had no explanation. This girl, Sam, had come out of nowhere and seemed to be immune to his influence over the world. He couldn't see what or who she really was. It was the first time in years that he had seen someone as everyone else sees them, in such a limited fashion. Normally Tom could look at a person, and whether or not he wanted to, he would see their whole life's history up to what they had for breakfast that day, and how it made them feel. Who could this girl be? Needless to say, the ego part of Tom was immediately enthralled with this new experience, or old experience rather, one that he had forgotten all about in the years of being one with everything.

"If you're not going to say it, I will," Sam said. She started mimicking his voice pattern jokingly to have a conversation with herself playing both parts, (something Tom was no stranger to) "Gee, I'd love to take a beautiful girl like you out to dinner tonight. Tee hee, that sounds wonderful, pick me up at six. All right, it's a date."

"Is it?" Tom asked.

"If you're not too busy floating here…"

"Not at all, I certainly want to go to dinner with you, and the store will be closed by then anyway." Tom got up off the ground and brushed himself off, trying to appear more professional.

"You won't be on the floor or under the table, during our date, will you? It will make our conversation harder."

"I make no promises," he said smiling, "maybe I'll even sit on the ceiling. Where should we go?"

"Where is there to go?" she asked.

That question struck him deeply, it was something he had heard before, something beyond the beyond. Farther along than the normal speech patterns of this plane. The meaning was there for Tom, but for who else? Where had he heard it before, and did she know the meaning of what she was saying?

"You mean we are already there," said Tom.

"No, I meant should we go to a nice restaurant or a local hotspot, that kind of thing. You really are a space cadet aren't you?"

"I am. Ground control to Major Tom and all… that's my name. Tom."

"Yeah, I got it. You know that song is completely over used, right?"

"Yes, but how many of them are really named Tom?"

"I'll tell you what, here is my number. Call me at 5:30 and I will tell you where you can pick me up," said Sam.

"I'm not used to this kind of suspense," Tom said, meaning the whole unknowing that he was experiencing at this point. Not being able to see his own future was new to Tom. What he said didn't mean quite so much to her, just that it was unusual not to have plans before carrying them out. She may have even thought that he was exaggerating playfully.

"Get used to it, but you better be as exciting as you seem, or I'm climbing out the bathroom window after eating lobster," she said to him.

"My life is very exciting, if you are open to it," he replied.

"I guess we'll find out tonight." She walked away leaving Tom standing there. He was floating a few inches above the ground, again. After a moment he came back to Earth, this time landing softly on his feet, and not his back.

"What a strange thing to have happen," Tom said to himself. Ordinary people may not think so, but ordinary people live ordinary lives. Something ordinary happening to someone extraordinary... that was new to Tom, but now he understood why he had been in the store in the first place. It hadn't been to buy groceries. It had been to meet her. Was it his subconscious that did this? Was it hers? Was it the universe toying with him?

Tom didn't have any answers, but quickly realized that he had to let go of the questions or risk being stuck in his ego for a moment longer. Desire. He had to avoid letting himself get sucked in. The more egoic he became, the less control he had over everything. It wasn't control as we see it, rather control as in the ability to adjust or alter. There could be no attachment to it. The moment Tom really desired one of his miracles to happen, was the moment ego would not allow it. He had to let go to gain this freedom.

Tom snapped his fingers and was back at home again, sitting on his front porch drinking coffee, his car parked nicely in the driveway.

'What should I do until then,' he thought to himself. I could just skip through time and not have to wait... but that would be offensive. Tom had the idea that skipping even a second of his life was an affront to existence. The whole purpose of existence was to exist. To deny that, or waste it in any way, was an insult. Hence, it was insulting to get wrapped up in mindly thoughts, because that kept him from being aware in the present moment.

He didn't hold on too tightly to this idea, but there was more of an attachment to it than he was willing to admit. It was because of this that he was so adverse to getting lost in the mind, and that is what allowed him to be one with everything... except Sam. There was mind again, always pointing out shortcomings. It wants to get a rise out of you. It wants to take you anywhere but here and now. "This coffee is amazing," Tom said to himself, then correcting his statement proceeded with, "this coffee is this coffee." Interpretation, categorization, and labeling, were of the mind. Associations. They could easily distract in a way that gets you involved. Tom didn't mind liking the coffee, it was getting involved with the feeling and attachment to liking that could become a problem. If he did or did not like the coffee, mind would bring up that memory the next time he drank coffee. He was perfectly happy with saying such things and moving on, but would often correct himself as a precaution so that it would be easier to stay focused. The moment you are unaware of the mind is the moment you get involved with it. Mind can be tricky.

Tom closed his eyes and became alert with all of his senses. He could hear the leaves rustling in the wind. He smelled the fresh earthiness of the coffee, and felt the cool wind of autumn on his skin. He knew what these things were but he did not identify them, he just enjoyed them with a silent mind. Stop labeling to help avoid comparing. He let out a deep breath of relaxation.

Tom was nervous about tonight. His date. He had a date. A real date, not one that he created. There was so little fun in controlling how a date went... no mystery or surprise knowing how everything would happen. Tom forgot what that was like until this moment, when he was literally feeling it in his body. He had a slight pressure in his head and chest. His heart rate was faster when he thought about it. His pupils dilated when visions of her danced through his head. It had been a long time since he liked anyone... in this way. He normally saw everyone as himself, something he had control over. Something that would happen however his mind made it happen, but it was not like that with her. She was separate from it.

Tom's mind was silent when he thought about it, simply because it couldn't comprehend this. There was no answer. No maybe this or maybe that, just silence after the question, 'why is she separate?' How could Tom have created a duality in his life after having been alone for this long? There was him and her. Not the him and him there had always been with everyone else. In fact, there normally wasn't either of them, just one and the same thing. The existence of everything was all the same, all one. How was she an exception to this rule? How was she dualistic?

"A good question indeed, everything is relative you know," said Albert Einstein who was sitting next to him on the porch drinking coffee as well.

"How can she be separate?" Tom asked him.

"She cannot be, it is all part of one grand unified force, you know this very well."

"Then how is this happening?"

"That is the pertinent question, isn't it? If it is all one and the same, how does it seem that she is not?" Einstein asked him.

"Does this not cause you suffering," asked Siddhartha, who was sitting on the porch cross-legged.

"This is a scientific matter," said Einstein, "the laws of the universe are being broken."

"You were starting to go down a spiritual path Einsteen," said Siddhartha, "it is my turn to discuss this now. Life is suffering, we must know the root of suffering and then we can go beyond it."

"I was here first, Buddha," said Einstein angrily, "and it is stein, not steen."

"He knows it is," said Tom, "but you are both here as my own creations and are reflected thusly based on my own knowledge and vision of you. Oneness. Thank you for trying to help, but if I don't know the answers myself, then I can't be given them through you."

"We are just trying to guide you," said Einstein.

"He must be ready to know the way, before we can teach it to him," said Buddha.

Both characters faded into nothingness and Tom sat there drinking his coffee with a silent mind.

As it got closer to 5:30, Tom decided to get ready for his date. It would be too fast to simply snap his fingers together and be ready, so he did it the old fashioned way and used his legs to walk to his bathroom and brush his teeth. He didn't want to have coffee breath on his first date with her, though there were much worse things to have on one's pallet. For a brief moment, Tom was caught by a glimpse of himself in the bathroom mirror. Tom hated seeing himself. It reminded him that he was cavorting around the world the same way everyone else was, stuck in this pile of flesh that was his body. Sure, he could change how he looked, but he still believed that he had no attachment to it, and therefore would leave it as it was meant to be. That is not to say that Tom was ugly, quite the contrary, he was quite ordinary looking, (above average, if anything). The problem was that to someone in his state of mind, he loathed the necessity of having an attachment to the body he occupied, though this was a necessary prerequisite for existing in this world.

When he looked in the mirror, he would stare into his own eyes, trying to see himself in there, but never getting past the surface. He never understood how this was him looking at himself. It felt so foreign. He would make faces at his reflection and try to forget that people saw him this way. He himself didn't see his face at all most of the time. It is a lesson of non-ego. Some cultures cover their mirrors to be reminded of this during times of loss. There is something greater than self. With a small mental struggle, Tom pulled himself away from the mirror and left the room.

It was time. Time to call. He took out his phone. Where was the number? He checked his pockets but couldn't find it. Tom closed his eyes then opened them again. The piece of paper with the number was in his hands. There had been a brief moment of worry before Tom used his power to manifest the number. What was happening to him? The world was trying to get in as always, but it was becoming more forceful as he was starting to have an attachment to what would happen. He could still brush it off now, but had not had such close calls for quite some time.

He stared at the phone as the number was entered and started to connect. He put it to his ear. Brrrr. Brrrr. Brrrr. Tom thought people would be able to identify the sound of the phone ringing if they had ever used one in their life, so it sufficed to have brrrr in place of the actual sound, which would make the book much more expensive, having an interactive sound unit just for this one easily recognized noise. If you are having trouble identifying, pick up your phone and call someone. Archaic technology says the children. Tom decided he should stop breaking the barrier of being a character in the book and someone who has an opinion about it, so he turned his attention back to the phone and what he was doing. He had been using this opportunity for the distraction from the slight anxiety he had been feeling, then the phone was answered.

"Hello?"

"Ahoy there!" said Tom, overly enthusiastically. He could practically hear her smirking on the other end of the line.

"This is either Tom, a pirate captain, or both. You would tell me if you were a pirate captain wouldn't you, Tom?"

"Argh, I swear me life on it, I ain't no sealubber."

"You are silly."

"That's why you're interested in me."

"Ah, who said I was?"

Tom didn't have a response for that one, so he stayed silent.

"Of course I'm interested," she said, "it's not every day that I give out my number to a stranger."

He breathed a sigh of relief. Though it should have been apparent to him that she was joking, it was rare that he found someone else with a similar sense of humor.

"I'm just glad you didn't try to make a joke about pirate's booty, it is overdone and too easy," she said.

"You didn't wait long enough. So, where should I pick you up?" She gave him the address. "What kind of car should I drive?" Tom asked.

"What, are you going to steal one?"

"Ha, no, I will create one that you like."

"Do we have time for that?"

"It takes no time at all."

"You and your parlor tricks... how about a yellow Lamborghini?"

"How about two?"

"Now I know you're messing with me. Just be here as soon as you can," Sam said.

Tom walked outside of his house with a big old grin on his face, and looked at his car. He snapped his fingers and it changed into a yellow Lambourgini. He didn't need to snap his fingers to make these things happen, it just seemed like something fun to do, like the girl on Bewitched who would wiggle her nose. Tom never saw himself as a witch, but what was the difference, beside the stigma attached to being a witch? He was sure many would be afraid of him if they knew what he could do, though he doubted he would ever meet any astronauts. (Tom mixed up the career of the husband on Bewitched with that of another similar TV show of the time, I Dream of Jeannie. Fans will know that the husband on Bewitched [Darrin], was an advertising Executive.) He is still upset that I left this in, but unlikely to admit it.

Upon getting in the car, Tom initially had no idea how to get to her house, but that didn't matter. All he needed was the address, and his mind.

Chapter 3
The Date

Tom didn't even start the car. He just closed his eyes and opened them in front of her house. The car was there with him. Still with the same mileage. Tom's understanding of this reality, took away the meaning of space and time. He got out of the car as Sam was running out of her house, "Oh my gosh, is that you?" Sam asked, "You got here so fast and I can't believe you got the car."

"To be honest I don't know where here is," Tom said, he closed his eyes for a moment and the information poured into his conscious mind, the exact map and details of how to get from his house to hers. It didn't make sense not to know. "I would have done a limousine myself, but your wish is my command madam," he said, opening the passenger door for her.

"You are something else," she said, taking his hand as she got into the car. As he was walking around the car to get in the driver's seat, Tom saw a figure out of the corner of his eye. He looked and there was no one there. It wasn't that out of the ordinary for this to happen, but for Tom it seemed to be occurring more frequently. It felt as if someone was staring at him. He shook off the feeling and got into the driver's seat, then took them to a nearby Vietnamese restaurant. It wasn't a particularly nice restaurant, or a place most people would choose for a first date, but Tom was convinced they had the best noodles. Sam didn't know what to do with him. He had come to her house in a car that was more expensive than most houses and then took her to this cheap noodle place.

"I'm having a hard time figuring you out," she said to him.

"Don't dwell on it, just have fun. That's what I do." They were sitting at the table with their noodles ready to have that awkward first date conversation that everyone has gone through at one point or another.

Tom always had his go-to question, not just for dates but for everyone, "If you could have anything in the world, what would it be?" he asked her.

"More time," said Sam.

"More time for what?"

"To do whatever I wanted. I feel like I'm always living a life that I have to live instead of the one I want to live."

"I know what you mean. How do you know you would use that time any better than the time you have now? The easy answer is to use what time you do have to do what you want, instead of wasting time wishing for more."

"You are the one who asked me."

"That's not what I meant," Tom said, "I mean it is, but you know, carpe diem, seize the day. What is stopping you from doing what you want in the time you have?" Tom asked.

"All kinds of things. I have bills to pay. I have to work so I can afford to live so I can keep paying health insurance, car insurance, and insurance insurance."

"Is that a thing?" Tom asked.

"No, but it should be, they are a nightmare to deal with."

"Those are reasons you don't have time, but they are holding you back. Believing in them, I mean. If you think they are holding you back, then they will hold you back. If you believe you are free and have plenty of time, then you will be. Let go of the attachment."

"I don't think it's that simple. If you want to be part of society, you have to follow their rules, and that means giving up most of your life for them and what they want," Sam said.

"I know it seems impossible, but as long as you think it is, it will be. I do have an easy way out for you though. I could get you more time if you wanted it, but there would be a catch."

"What kind of catch? Is this another one of your parlor tricks?"

"No, but the catch is, you would have to spend a lot of that time with me."

"Ha! What a curse. I don't know how I would manage. So, are you going to do that for me? Give me more time?"

"I can't do it myself, my power doesn't seem to work on you, but there is someone who can. The same man who came to me when I needed help."

"I still don't know if I believe any of this, even if you are cute. Is this when the truth comes out and you ask me to join a cult?"

"You think I'm cute?"

"That's what you took from that?"

"I'm can't tell if you really believe me, though it's not really that important..." Tom said.

"That's right, it's not important. All that matters is that I do like you and I'm here with you now."

"It's interesting you know, most people ask for money, power, fame, all kinds of unfulfilling things. More time could be a blessing, if it was used properly."

"Those are very limited views of what is important. The most important thing to me is to enjoy life, but not at anyone else's expense. The world is big enough for all of us to be happy if we allow ourselves."

"Perfect! You are right. One hundred percent. That is beautiful. I love it," Tom said, raising his water glass for a toast.

"Are you making fun of me?"

"No, on the contrary. How are the noodles?"

"What, you're changing the subject?"

"No no no, well, yes, but not for the reason you think I am. I just wondered if the food is as good as I think it is."

"It's okay, I'm just messing with you."

"Oh, that's real cute. I see you're full of surprises too. Want to see something fun? I can have our waiter come over here and read poetry or sing show-tunes."

"Is that how you impress people? No, of course not. That wouldn't be very nice at all, think of how he would feel. Making him do something like that."

"He would do it willingly. I can get him anything he wants."

"I think he just wants us to eat, tip and leave," Sam said.

"I have to admit something. I don't know how to impress you. I am not used to it."

"The best way is to stop trying and just be yourself. I don't know if you can do all of the things you claim or not, but it doesn't matter to me. I just want to get to know you."

"It has been so long for me. I haven't felt allowed to be me... it just doesn't seem like anyone cares who I am, you know? It is always what I can do for them that I focus on..."

"Well I'm different. I am interested in you, not what you can do."

"Will you help me to do this right?"

"Yes, I will silly, let's start simple, how old are you?"

"I... I don't know."

"What do you mean, you don't know? When were you born?" Sam asked.

"I can't remember. There is something holding me back from thinking about it. The last time I remember I was in my twenties, I don't know early or late, my memory of it seems to be gone."

"Were you in an accident?"

"I don't know. When I try to think about it, it hurts, in my heart, there is something that won't let me think about it."

"I'm sorry. I don't mean to bring up bad memories."

"It's okay, I don't quite understand it myself. I know that you weren't saying it to hurt me."

"Do you really know that?" Sam asked.

"I'm giving you the benefit of the doubt. It is hard enough not being able to read you as it is."

"Maybe I am the one who erased your memories!"

"Come on, that's not funny. Why would anyone do a thing like that?"

"I wouldn't. That sounds excruciating. I could never do that to someone. I can't imagine who would... no matter how bad things got. Would you?"

"Would I what?"

"Would you erase someone's memories if you could?"

"I can."

"You can?" Sam asked.

"Yes, but no, I would never do it. Having had to live like this for so long... I could never put someone through it. It is horrible. Nothing can possibly justify it. There are limits to what one should and shouldn't do, given the power." Sometimes the real power is in holding back.

"I'm glad you feel that way. What kind of a person would do that?"

"I don't know. I'm sorry this was brought up. What else can we talk about?" Tom asked. It was getting to be too much for him. His lost memories were a touchy subject because he couldn't do anything about it. It was easy to drop attachment to things he could control, but things he had no power over, especially such intimate things as his own lost memories, were hard for him to think about.

"What do you like to do for fun, I mean beside floating and staring at the ceiling," she said, giving him a sly grin.

"That's more entertainment than fun. I do a lot of that kind of thing, fly my car here and there, make things explode then reappear normal, walk through walls, all kinds of things."

"All kinds of parlor tricks?"

"Boy, you really make this sound mundane."

"It is! What are you accomplishing with all of that? If I had that kind of power I would use it to help people, or at least make them feel a little better about having to live in this society," Sam said.

"That's what I like about you. If it were that easy I would. There was a time when I tried. I wanted the same thing, but learned the hard way that it is not up to me whether people are happy or not. It is up to them. It is not what they have or don't have, it is a state of mind. That is one thing I could never permanently change about anybody. They would always revert back to themselves in the end no matter how much I did for them. The biggest thing I learned is that wanting doesn't make you happy, and getting what you want makes you even less happy. At least when you are wanting, there is hope that something exists that can make you happy. When you get it, then there is no more hope that it will. Then you have to move on to something else to want, or dwell on being unhappy, but no longer thinking there is something that can change it."

"That sounds awful. I think I know what you mean though," Sam said.

"I'm sorry, this must be awful first-date conversation. It has been a long time for me."

"Me too. I used to love someone, a long time ago. You remind me of him. I held on to the idea that nothing else would make me happy. The truth is, I wanted my own memory of him, not who he really was. I couldn't accept him for who he had become. I have tried to block it out except for the lesson I learned. No one can make you happy but yourself. For me, seeing other people happy makes me happier because being able to ease their suffering, even for a brief amount of time, is more valuable to me than all the riches of the world," Sam said.

Everything changed. Tom was no longer sitting at the table eating noodles. Something had transported him through time and space. There was a song playing, people dancing all around, "faded, wasted..." he couldn't make out the lyrics. The vibrations of the bass were playing so loudly they shook his whole body, it was addictive, "All I want to do is try not to... faded... wasted, baby, I'm fading." He had gotten lost. What was he doing. The world was vibrating. His consciousness was blurred by something he had taken. What a beautiful song, his mind said to him. It was hard to have control at this point. What had he done? How had he gotten here? He was slouched into a couch, watching Sam dancing to the beat. She wasn't dancing with anyone. He was practically hypnotized watching the way she moved, perfectly with the flow of everything. He wasn't sure if this was good or not, but she was still there, and that is what mattered most to him in the moment.

Sam looked at him, "Are you okay over there?"

"What is this!" Tom practically had to yell to be heard. She could tell what he was trying to say the third time he yelled because she put her ear an inch away from his mouth.

"I told you it would have an effect on you, babe," she said. Sam straddled his legs and sat on top of him so they were face to face. She seemed to be dealing with this a lot more easily than he was, if she had taken the same thing. She gently caressed his face pushing his hair back out of the way.

"You have to let go," she said to him. Tom was having the hardest time dealing with this, not being under the influence of... whatever this was, but finding himself in these places without knowing how he had gotten there. Sometimes his ego would rebel and take over without his knowledge... he thought that was what had happened. Most people know that mind follows body, if there is something you want, mind will create it for you at whatever cost.

Then he let go. The feeling had gotten so intense that the only thing left to do, was to stop holding on. The pressure was released, he felt at ease. Tom took a deep breath and then noticed that Sam was kissing him. It made sense. Why else would someone get on top of you in such a fashion. Tom loved this, that kind of raw passion, the intensity, the will to power.

"I bet you didn't see this coming," Sam said to him. Before he had time to answer, she was kissing him again. He hadn't seen it coming. That was because a minute ago he was being awkward on a first date in a dingy Pho restaurant. Was it even the same night? This was the cost of the wish he had made. He always got what he wanted... even if he wasn't there to remember it.

"Tom! Tom!" Sam was shaking him. He was back at the restaurant with noodles hanging out of his mouth.

"What?" he said.

"Are you okay? You were sitting there spaced out. Where did you go?"

"Somewhere beautiful. You were there too... I mean, you will be," he replied.

"What do you mean?"

"Nothing. I just saw something that hasn't happened yet. The weird part is wondering whether it will happen because I saw it or if I saw it because it would happen."

"You are so weird."

"I might be."

"Don't worry, I think it's cute," she said. Tom smiled at her. Tonight was going to be incredible.

"So, you were telling me about someone who could make my wish come true," Sam said.

"I was going to, yes. I still am, but there is a longer story I have to go into first. I can't remember how long ago it was, it feels like a lifetime. I haven't been the same person since then, at least. I wasn't in a good place back then. I had just finished school and had been living on my own for a little less than a year when I realized that things weren't going the way they were supposed to. When I was young, everyone told me what I should do in order to get where I was supposed to be, according to their idea of the universe. I should be someone with a steady job, a nice family and overall, a very happy person. I was disillusioned by reality at this point. The jobs I had chosen over my own happiness had all felt wasteful. They didn't come anywhere near what I wanted to do or the potential I always thought I had. I was just listening to one person after another and getting nowhere. I didn't want to spend my life as an errand boy or slave and that is how I felt. Working for other people who didn't care in the slightest who I was or what I wanted. I met countless numbers of sheep-people who all said and did the same thing, listening to the old news instead of wanting something new and bigger. I cringed every time I had to present a project to a client, or my boss, who only liked my ideas when she repeated them as her own. It felt like I was wasting my life, living someone else's life. I couldn't stand it.

So I did the impossible. I gave it all up. I stopped working and started living my own life the way I wanted it. It was a much harder lifestyle, but it felt more real and free than anything I had yet experienced. I had nobody to own up to, no one to report to. Nothing that others wanted of me. I spent my free time thinking and working on my own creative projects. For the first time I could read in peace without feeling like I was missing a deadline or procrastinating.

Everything up until this point had made me feel like I was wrong, and now I finally felt like life was right. That is when I met my guru. Not guru in the way that you probably think of one, it has such a stigma these days. A guru is not someone who will show you the way, a guru is the way. He led me to the lifestyle that I am leading now. He helped me to let go of everything I was still holding on to, to make peace with what I had been and wanted to be. He showed me that it was all okay no matter how it seemed. It was just a matter of perspective. Many people were happy being told what to do and having no say, and that is why he had come to me. He knew that I was not satisfied in the life I had been given, the path I had followed, and where it led me. He told me that I would be granted one wish, to use it wisely, that it could either bring my life to a much higher level or pull me down to nothing.

I don't know how much of it I believed at the time, but I considered it carefully and decided what I would wish for. I told him that I wanted the ability to see and change everything, the universal existence, from the smallest atom to the largest of monuments, to know all and bend it to my will. He chuckled at my wish but told me it would be granted. He had been given a similar wish when his lord asked him if he wished to become one with him. He had said no, because he would no longer be able to serve him if they were one in the same, even though there was no separation anyway. He gave me his blessing and told me that I would have to let go of my attachments for the wish to come to fruition. It wasn't easy, and I don't know if I believed him at first, but then things started to happen as I willed them. I started to know what people were thinking, what would happen and has happened. It filled my mind, like there had been a void all along. I quickly understood that the only time it didn't work was when I cared too much, when I was too attached to the outcome. If I was calm and peaceful with it, letting what was meant to be happen, everything shifted toward my thinking. Thus the fork becomes a spoon, becomes a straw, becomes a flower." Tom had been holding a fork, which transformed into all of these shapes and then into the rose, which he handed to Sam.

"I can't tell if you are serious or just a glorified magician," Sam said.

"It's a little bit of both."

"Do you want to get out of here? There is a club down the street that plays the best music."

"You read my mind. It has already happened, and now will manifest."

"One more thing, how do I find that man to make my wish?" Sam asked.

"Ha. You don't. He will only let you find him when you are ready to let go."

"Alright then, enough existentialism for now, let's have some fun."

She got up from the table and pulled him away by the hand. The next thing Tom knew, he was waking up with his arms around her, and her long blonde hair in his face. He didn't move. There was too much to consider at this point before deciding what to do. She was fast asleep, after all. He didn't remember how he had gotten there or what had happened after the couch but he had his suspicions.

This was all new to Tom. To beat a dead horse, it had been a long time since anything surprising and new had happened to him. Tom had conflicting emotions of comfort, peace, rest, liveliness, and fear. Most of him was happy with where he had ended up, even though he didn't remember how he had gotten there. Memory was a sore-spot for Tom. He struggled with what it meant that he couldn't remember conceivably important parts of his life.

Should he wait until she wakes up? Should he leave? Did she want him to stay? Was it his choice? This was so weird and new to Tom. Everything had been under his thumb until he had met this girl who was immune to his control over everything. He so desperately wanted to let go and simply be in the moment. It was so pleasurable to have her in his arms, like he was living a normal life with this beautiful girl, but what if she faded away?

Then she woke up. But she didn't get up and leave. She turned around and faced him. It seemed that she felt the same way he did.

"I had a really good time last night," she said to him.

'Isn't that supposed to be my line?' he asked himself. After all, he was in her bed. She kissed him gently on the nose.

"It is about time we met," she said.

Tom knew better than to ask her what had happened last night. It was best just to assume that whatever it was had been meaningful and fun for both of them.

"I really liked your story, Tom, but tell me, if one were really inclined to find the man who gave you these powers, where would they begin?" Sam asked.

"I already told you, if you are ready, he will find you."

"I remember what you said, I was just wondering, if you really needed to see him, how would you go about looking?"

"Me personally? I would will it. He gave me that power. I know I have no control over him, but I believe he would allow me to see him again. For those who are searching, I would start in the most desolate of places, where there are no distractions. People like that abhor technology and anything that is disruptive to the energy around them. They like pure spaces where people question less, and believe more.

I would look in the most underdeveloped of countries, where there is the most pure suffering from innocent people who know no other life. A place where people are happy with their lives and with what they have. They are the most free because they accept what is, what has been given, without question, without wanting, but have not been misled the way we have in this technological, money driven world. Are you interested in meeting him?"

"Why wouldn't I be after the way you spoke of him?"

"I understand it can be tempting, but you have to realize that the more you get, the more you will want. If you are given one thing, you will want ten. It is an endless cycle of desire and attachment. The key to being happy in life is to accept what you have as what you want instead of wanting what you don't have. I promised you I could get you what you wanted and I will keep that promise, but you must hold me at my terms. It is my desire to spend that time with you, then you will never know want or need again. This will be your choice, not just to spend that time with me, but to give up want, attachment, desire, need, all of it. You will always be blessed with more than you desire if you desire less than you are given. It takes a loss of self, but this is not a real loss because self is something created, not something real. Do you think this is something you would be able to do?"

"It seems a little sudden... I think so, yes. I want to spend the rest of my life with you. I know this sounds crazy, we only met yesterday, but I feel like we understand each other and have our best interests at heart. He kissed her on the forehead and closed his eyes. This was some vision of heaven on earth for him. He fell asleep still holding her in his arms, face to face, a beautiful scene.

Chapter 4
The Saint

Sam had traveled many miles, for many years, searching for the guru. Her wish was of utmost importance to her and her vision of how the world should be. It was a long and tiresome day of searching in a desert wasteland. Almost out of water, Sam approached a small village that seemed to appear out of nowhere. She was greeted by the head of the village.

"What do you want?" he asked her.

"I am here to see the guru," she replied.

"What guru?"

"You know the guru I mean."

"The Saint?"

"Yes, please give me audience with him."

"He doesn't want to see you."

"Please, I need to see him. I must talk to him."

"He says you are here for the wrong reasons and that you should come back when you are pure of heart."

"Please, I have come such a long way, you must let me see him." The man closed his eyes and seemed to be in a meditative state. After a few minutes, he opened his eyes and seemed a bit perturbed. Whatever he had been doing in that state seemed to have changed his mind.

"All right. You may be allowed to be in his presence, but don't be surprised if he kicks you out right away," he said.

She cautiously followed the man, walking behind him through hot sand with very thin sandals. Soon they were at a large temple. The door was at least five times taller than she was. It was opened before them, and the man led her through the great halls to the main place of worship.

A hundred feet away on a small wooden bed sat an old man in a blanket. There emanated a beautiful song-like chanting from this man of white light, even though his mouth was not moving: "Shree Ram, Hare Ram, Shree Ram, Hare Ram." The universe was singing around him. He was in a trance-like state. Sam felt she would be bothering him to interrupt this state, so she sat down in front of him and joined in. Even though the shree and hare exchanged places at an unknown interval, she somehow managed to be in tune with him.

"Shree, Hare Shree, Hare Hare Rammmmm, Hare Ram, Shree Ram, Hare Ram, Ram Ram Hare Shree, Shree Ram, Hare Ram, Shree Ram." One of the man's eyes cracked open to see who had joined him, even though he was already conscious of it all. He was playing a game.

"Ahhh, you know Ram too?" he asked her.

"I'm afraid I don't," said Sam.

"He knows you!"

She felt a warmth spread all over her body, starting from her heart. There were tears coming to her eyes as she felt the tremendous love coming from this being. "Ram, Ram, Ram, Hare Ram, Ram Ram," the man continued for some time. She joined in once again.

"Ram Ram Ram."

"Very good!" he said. "He can hear you, you know? He is right here with us, all of the time. It is our duty to serve him."

"I will do my best," Sam replied, "but to be honest, there is another reason I came."

"You didn't come here for Ram? That is okay, he is everywhere. You need not go anywhere to find Ram, he is always with you in your heart." The man held up one finger to her heart and she felt an even more intense surge of love, warmth, and energy vibrating through her whole body. Tears were flowing from her eyes. They had no emotional source but love.

"Tut, tut, I know why you are here," he said to her, "you want something from me, don't you?"

"It is true, I have come here to ask you for something."

"Your wish, right? You have a wish to make from me. You want more time, don't you? More time for God?"

"No. Yes... and no. That is what I wanted when I came here, but there is something that I must ask for instead, for someone else that I care about. It is more important than what I want. I want to see and change everything."

"NAHIN! HELP! No! This is not your wish. These are stolen words. You cannot have his wish. You know it is not yours," he said, shaking his finger at her.

"I thought you could do anything," she said.

"Nahin! I don't do anything! God does everything. I will not dishonor his name in this way. Make your own request or get out!"

"Alright. I know what it is I want."

"So does he. Why did you come here? What did you think you could do in the face of God? Your men will never find us. He loves you so much and I can see you love him too. How could you do this to him?"

"Are you going to grant me my wish or not?"

"I will, but not for you, because someone else needs it more than you do, and there will be a cost."

"You sound just like him. I have already suffered more than any cost that you could impose upon me. What is it that I have to do in order to fulfill this wish?"

"It is already done. The cost is not one I have imposed upon you, but one you were destined for. It is part of your incarnation. You will have to love him."

Sam didn't reply for a minute, thinking about what he was trying to tell her, knowing it had already happened.

"If it is already done," she said, "please grant my wish."

"Alright mother, what is it that you wish?"

"My wish is that..."

Chapter 5
Betrayal

"Don't even try it," said Sam, standing over the bed, where Tom was handcuffed. There were people in black suits all around the apartment, clearly from some government agency.

"What is this?" Tom asked, playing along to see where it would go.

"You think you could just waltz back into my life and pretend everything was different? You're lucky if you really don't remember what happened last time, if that is your excuse, but you can't take it away. It happened. I don't know if you really are innocent or just stupid to come back here like this, but we can't let you do what you've been doing, taking control over people as if they were puppets.

We've created a way that you can't see our thoughts, our lives, our minds. You won't be able to do anything as long as you are wearing those handcuffs. We are going to find your guru and stop you for good. You think it is okay to force your will upon others? You are disgusting. This little mouse was given a cookie and he keeps on wanting and wanting. You are sick, Tom. You can't just do whatever you want to whomever you want. There are rules that dictate this society. The people have a right to be who they are, not who you want them to be," Sam said, concluding her speech of righteousness.

"I don't have a say in this, do I?" Tom asked.

"No. You have shown your true self and that is something that cannot be allowed in this society. We are going to find your guru and stop all of this. Nobody should be allowed to have the power that you have been given."

"You think you can hurt him?" Tom asked smiling. "You don't know what you're in for. You think that I have power over anything? It is nothing compared to his connection with the divine. I am just a servant of a servant. You will gain nothing."

"We gained something... we have you. That is the first step to getting him. If I were you, I would cooperate."

"My dear Sam, I may not remember anything of my past, and it sounds like you know more than I do about it. I will do anything to help you if you let me back in. I know you don't trust me for whatever reason and want to see me suffer for something that I have done. I don't know if it is just or not, but I will give you the benefit of the doubt. We can have a long and full life together, with all the time in the world if you let go of this obsession to stop me and my guru. My wants are only for the benefit of us both. You and me. I do not wish to see other's suffer by my hand or anyone else's. I don't see my life as complete without you, and I know there is a part of you that feels the same way. I am left with nothing to do but beg you once more to see things clearly so that all may be so," said Tom.

"Shut your mouth. You speak lies and blasphemies. I know you and your manipulative ways. You think these memories were erased because of what I did? They were because of what you did. Things I will never forget. When I asked you if you would be strong enough to erase someone else's memories, I already knew the answer, because you refused to do it for me after leaving yourself a blank slate, you coward. You took the suffering away from yourself and left me to deal with what you did to me."

"Please. If there is something I can do to make this right, I beg of you to ask it of me. I will do what I can to keep things just and support truth," said Tom.

"There is nothing you can do. We will find him and we will decide what happens from here on out," said Sam.

Tom shook his head and sighed. They had not learned anything. Any of them. He had been trying to tell them, but they would be dooming themselves if they continued upon this path. Maybe he should erase their memories. At least then the playing field would be level. Would that be a good thing to do? Not good as in good or bad, right or wrong, but as in just. Would there be any merit in it? They said he did it to himself, and if he was willing to do it to himself, why would it be that much worse to do it on other people? They said he would have no control with these handcuffs on. Tom didn't know if they knew they were bluffing, but he knew that the power he had would not be limited so easily. At the same time, he wanted to see where this was going to take him, so he did not resist, did not teleport himself to a remote island where he could enjoy a tropical drink with the sun shining down on him as the ocean spray gently caressed his legs.

"I hope you do find him," Tom said, "if anyone can help you, it is him."

"Take him to the holding cell," Sam said, talking to the sharply dressed men who nodded with acknowledgment of the order instead of speaking. They took him by the arms and dragged him to the black truck that was waiting outside.

"Would have been nice if you guys had given me a pair of pants," Tom mumbled to himself as they threw him into the back seat of the car, wearing only his boxers. When the two agents got in the car, Tom was already dressed in a suit, his hands were no longer handcuffed, but in his lap. The agents were at alert, but he told them to relax, and that he would cooperate as long as it was in his best interest. Reluctantly they joined him in the car and drove on to their holding facility.

"Should we report this?" one of the agents asked the other.

"No," said the other, "she needs to stay focused."

They took him to their facility where he was taken deep underground and put into a decently sized cell. The contents were very limited at the start, but Tom quickly visualized and manifested that which he wanted to keep him occupied. Mostly books that were on his reading list and could keep him busy without making the guards too anxious. He assumed they did not report his miraculous escape from nudity and the handcuffs that were supposed to subdue him, so that the higher ups did not consider them inept. They were taking a chance on him and he appreciated that, knowing full well he could leave any time he wanted. All that he had heard of this was when he first entered the building and the guards said that Tom was under enough sedation without the handcuffs, so that the officers were not suspicious of their entrance.

The agents claimed they had searched him and that it was Sam's orders for them to leave him in this outfit. Tom had connected the dots that they meant Sam when they said agent something or other. It rang a bell deeper in his memory than was available to him. When Tom heard familiar words, memories were unlocked of what had happened to him. This one in particular, Agent [REDACTED] brought him to a beachfront location in Malibu. The same place he had been in his imagined life on the beach. This time in his mind, she was there with him. Who was he? This erased memory was just a small part of a bigger story that made up his secret life. Not secret to them, secret to him.

In a comfortable chair next to Tom sat Einstein once again.

"This is indeed a pickle," said Einstein in his German accent.

"I don't know that it's a scientific matter," Tom replied, "this may be best suited for someone else."

"You know it is you who brought me here?"

"I do. You are a voice of reason, and I couldn't think of anyone else."

A new voice came from the room, not from anybody in particular, it sounded as though it were coming from the universe itself all around him. Was he doing this?

"Uh-oh. I better leave. The big man is coming," said Einstein quickly disappearing.

"Ram Ram Ram," the voice all around him continued, filled his very core with warmth and love. Tom got to his knees and put his head down toward where the guru was appearing.

"I saw your friend!" said the guru.

"You did? What did she want, beloved Bhagwan?"

"She was thinking of you."

"Thinking of me? I don't think she is very happy with me."

"She loves you, you know. Do you love me?"

"Of course, I love you."

"You want me to get you out of here?"

"No, that isn't necessary. I can leave whenever I want," Tom said, knowing that he was only playing along with him.

"You know you are not supposed to use these powers for yourself. What would you do without your abilities?"

"I wouldn't do anything, I would keep you in my heart as I do now."

"Ha ha ha! You are a good one, Tom. You must forgive her when she asks."

"I'm not upset with her, what is there to forgive her for?"

"Wait until she asks. Then you must. Will you do this for me?"

"Of course I will, anything you ask will be done."

Chapter 6
The Release

"Who is he talking to in there?" asked one of the guards to the other while watching the video monitor of Tom's cell.

"Beat's me, the guy creeps me out," replied the other. Sam entered the facility and filled out the paperwork for the release of Prisoner 7190, or as we know him, Tom.

"Are you sure you want to do this? He is a threat to national security," said the officer who had gotten the paperwork ready.

"He is no threat, he is just an idiot," said Sam, "a selfish idiot."

Sam walked up to the cell where Tom was being held, and shook her head at the decorations he had put up.

"You couldn't even take jail seriously, could you?" she said to him.

"What do you mean?" Tom asked.

"You're always showing off, couldn't you just stay in a plain jail cell for a few weeks? Why did you even stay?"

"You wanted me to."

"I know I did, but you can go now, you haven't broken any laws. I can't hold you here just because of how I feel about you, as much as I want to."

"You're releasing me?"

"You were never held captive anyway, just get out of here."

"I stayed for you. Come with me."

"Tom… I don't know if I can even look at you right now. You don't know what it's like having to see someone who hurt you so badly and doesn't even know they did anything wrong. As long as you don't have your memories, I can't be around you, but if you did have them... then you might become the person who hurt me. I leave that choice up to you." She handed him an envelope. "Look at this when you are ready to know what happened, or just do the smart thing and burn it, then forget you ever met me."

"Let go of you? That's easier said than done. I didn't even know you a few weeks ago... as far as my memory serves. Somehow we were brought together again. It has to be more than coincidence."

"It's nothing, Tom, just leave me alone. I was happier before I ever met you."

"Sam, I can tell there is something between us, why won't you help me to understand it?"

"Because it hurts! You hurt me! You don't know the things you did and how that made me feel. You act like you have all the power in the world but you won't use it to help the people you love."

Sam waved her hands toward Tom, and to both of their surprise, Tom was immediately transported out of the jail cell and onto the floor of his living room. Sam had powers? What!?! The guru said she had visited him, but not what she had asked for. The letter was on the couch next to him. Tom got up from the ground, dusting himself off once again, still surprised with what had happened. He didn't really know where the space dust came from (that's what he called it), but every time he traveled that way there was a thin layer of dust, much like being in New Mexico. He took the letter in his hands and looked at it. It was just an ordinary letter... or so it seemed. Should he look at it? He had to. It had been paining him that he didn't know parts of his own life. Especially if it had hurt Sam. Though he had only known her briefly, there was some connection between them that was greater than their night together.

'You can just leave that here and get away,' said a voice in his head. It was his ego again, trying to keep him distracted, 'just drop it and go have fun. Live however you want.' Tom knew he couldn't do that, no matter how appealing it sounded. He would live the rest of his life suffering from the bit of knowledge that there was so much being hidden from him. He would have to open the letter.

He unfolded the flap, which had been stuck into the envelope to keep the contents from spilling out. He pulled out a folded 8.5" x 11" piece of paper. Unfolding it, he noticed that there was only one word on it, in the middle of the page.

APERTAMBUXTION

Chapter 7
The Other Side

Tom looked at the word with some confusion. "What?" he said aloud to nobody in particular, then spoke the word, "Apertambuxtion?" The room was filled with white light. Everything in the house that Tom was familiar with was now gone and replaced by a white void. He was in an empty space, somewhere between worlds.

A man wearing a cloak walked up to him out of the nothingness and spoke, "Welcome."

"What is this? Where am I? Who are you?" Tom shot out his questions without waiting for an answer.

"So many questions for someone without attachment," replied the man, "my name is John. I am like you, someone who can bend the universe at will. I am here to help you get your memories back. We were brought here because you read the letter. It was created as part of your memory wipe. The memories had to go somewhere, so they were sealed here along with the letter. When you take away memories, they are kept in an in-between space. A bridge for both of our worlds. The memories needed an arbiter, so to speak. I was chosen to be the one who would return your memories when you wanted them back. Everyone must accept who they are, who they have been, and what they have done. It was only a matter of time before I expected you back here again."

"I was here before?" Tom asked.

"You have been here a few times, actually. There were times when you had small memories removed, and a few major times when we made you into the man you are today. You were not happy with yourself, Tom. Don't take it lightly that you had these memories removed. Someone willing to go to that extreme must have had a good reason for it.

Furthermore, we cannot simply restore the memories of Sam, and I know that is what you want. If we restore your memories, it is going to bring back all of your memories. You may find yourself becoming someone that you don't like. We won't be able to remove your memories again after this, it is too much of a risk. If you get them back, they will be here to stay."

"I want to do it," Tom said.

"I know you do, but please, take a few minutes while we are preparing, and consider this more thoughtfully. I know you won't have Sam if you don't bring back these memories, but you don't know if you will have her afterward either. It is a chance you are taking, and you may not like where you end up."

"I understand," Tom said. How bad could it be? He had been so busy suffering from not remembering that he had never considered what could possibly make him want to enter into that state willingly. He was about to find out. "If there is a chance for Sam and I to be together, I am willing to take it. I don't know why I feel so strongly about her, but I know my memories will explain everything."

"You take the good with the bad kind of thing?" John asked.

"Yes."

"Alright then. I am ready when you are, but remember, once it has started it cannot be stopped. If you try to end the process before it is complete, it would jeopardize your entire memory. All of it this time. I am not trying to scare you, I am only telling you this because I don't want to deal with you as a vegetable. One more thing I forgot to mention, with these memories comes ego. If there were attachments you erased in these memories, and they are brought back now, they will be stronger than ever. That means you will have no control over these attachments. Your powers will not be anywhere near as effective as they are now."

"I would give up everything for her," Tom said.

"Hmm. I only wish you had said that last time. All of this could have been avoided. It was nice to meet this version of you, Tom, always a pleasure to connect with kindred spirits. Don't forget the person you are now. He is an ideal version of you. When the process is over you will wake up in your bedroom. Are you ready? This is your last chance to change your mind."

"I am ready. Do it."

"I know you are. You have always been one to stick by your feelings when they are strong. That can be an integral part of a personality. Close your eyes."

Tom listened and closed his eyes, now seeing only darkness, waiting for something to happen. He opened them, ready to tell John that it wasn't working, but when he did, Tom was no longer in the white space. He was in his childhood bedroom lying in bed with the sheets pulled up over his head. He was a young boy, but he had his adult mind and could now understand the yelling coming from downstairs that he had been afraid of as a child. His parents were fighting. This must have been before his dad left them. It came back to Tom's mind that this had been part of his childhood. His dad had left them when he was young. He heard the sound of glass breaking, the fight was getting more intense. Tom got out of his bed and crept down the stairs trying not to be seen. He was working his way

49

through the memory. Tom had walked in on his parents while they were arguing. His mother was the first to notice him there.

"Stop it! We can't fight in front of our child," said his mother. She was holding a knife behind her back. Tom had seen it briefly before she turned around when he walked in. She had been using it to defend herself.

"You mean your child. How do I even know he's my son?" his father yelled back at her.

"Why do you do this to us? Can't you come home sober for just one night and spend time with us as a family."

His father was angry and drunk. Tom could see why this memory had been blocked. It was cold and hard, nothing a child should be part of. His father was done arguing with her. He wrestled the knife out of her grasp and threw her to the ground. Tom ran up to him in an effort to pull them apart, "Stop, don't hurt mommy," he said in his childhood voice. He was too small to do anything.

His father swung his arm at Tom, hitting him across the face. Tom was thrown to the ground. Everything became fuzzy. The world was spinning and he wasn't sure if there had been a moment of blackness before he could see what was happening again, but he knew that his head was bleeding from where it had hit the ground. He could feel the warm liquid running down the side of his forehead. His mother was screaming now, knowing that her baby was hurt.

"Get out! Get out of my house!" she yelled, but he wasn't ready to leave.

"I'm not going anywhere," said his father, stepping toward them, "until I teach both of you some respect."

"Stop," said Tom, standing up. The house started shaking. Was there an earthquake, or was it just their house? Tom stared at his father with pain and hatred in his eyes, knowing now from an adult state of mind how horrible this really had been. Tom held out his hand toward the man who claimed to love them. His mother watched, feeling her heart beating even faster at what was happening, praying it would all go away. His father was a foot off the ground holding his hands to his own neck.

"Stop him. You freak, get your hands off of me," his father choked out.

Tom waved his hand and sent his father flying across the room into the wall. He fell to the ground gasping, rubbing his throat where the invisible force had held him.

"You are going to pay for that," his father said, "nobody treats me this way, especially not some kid." His father got up and started to run toward Tom, but his mother tackled him before he could get near her child again. There was silence as Tom's mother lay on top of his now still father. He wasn't going to get up again. She had picked up the knife before she tackled him, and it was no longer an empty threat. After a moment of consideration for what had just happened, his mother sat up and looked at Tom.

"How did you do that?" she asked him through her tears. "You were supposed to be in bed."

The memory ended. Tom didn't know where he was. Everything was dark. His breathing was rapid. He held his hand up to his head, it didn't hurt anymore. His mother had pleaded self-defense so that she could take care of her only son. She would always be there for him when he needed her, though when he got old enough, he would run away from her, breaking her heart for the second time. Tom was spoiled for the rest of his childhood. He got everything he wanted. When he didn't, that made him angry, and when he was angry, bad things would happen. Were these really Tom's memories, or had he been altering them by reliving them? Was it possible for him to change what had happened while reliving it? These were supposed to be memories, so how could he alter them? The carefree and loving person that Tom thought he always had been, was being replaced by the truth.

A new scene came into his vision. This time he was in high school. There was a group of kids ganging up on another student.

"What did I tell you about staying away from him?" Tom asked them.

"What are you going to do about it, freak?" said the (presumably) head bully. The others laughed. They took their attention away from the kid on the ground and made a circle around Tom.

"You should mind your own business," said the bully, "or you might get hurt."

"You're making a big mistake," said Tom.

"You made the mistake," said the bully before he took a swing at Tom to punch him, but his arm was stopped in mid-air.

"What are you doing?" asked one of the other kids, "Hit him!" They looked on confused and terrified as the head bully put his arm down and stood straight up like a board. His eyes rolled back in his head and his mouth started leaking drool. His whole body was convulsing. One of the other kids tried to grab Tom, but was thrown against the lockers grasping at his neck.

"Tom! What is going on here?" one of the teachers had walked in on the situation. Tom released the two students.

They both fell to the ground, but would get up with only minor physical injury.

"I think he was having a seizure," said Tom, casually walking away. "You better send him to the doctor." The other kids ran as the teacher helped the boy off the ground. Tom left the scene again. He was going somewhere else in the memories he had lost.

He was back at school again, but it was after hours. He was waiting for his ride home when a girl with blonde hair walked up to him.

"Hi," she said.

"Hi," Tom replied. She was cute. He had seen her around before but had never imagined working up the courage to talk to her. Even with the kind of power Tom possessed, there was still that same fear holding him back from taking what he wanted in life. Tom was afraid of himself sometimes, like even he didn't know what he was capable of. He used that as an excuse not to pursue the girl he liked.

"I'm Sam," said the girl.

"My name is Tom," said Tom.

"Thank you for helping my brother. Those bullies have been leaving him alone thanks to you."

"I didn't do it for him," said Tom, "it was the right thing to do. These kids think they are better than others, that they can control them just because they are bigger and stronger. It's not right. Real strength comes from helping people in need. From doing what is right and just."

"Well, thank you anyway. He means the world to me. He has been picked on most of his life and you are the first one to stand up for him," Sam said.

"I would do it again in a heartbeat."

Everything went black again. Tom had spent his youth with his new best friend, Adam, and Adam's little sister, Sam. The three of them could always be found together. As they grew up, Tom and Sam started dating. It had been unplanned, but one night while they were hanging out, Adam had to leave and one thing led to another. Tom and Sam had started kissing. She had always admired him and he had always felt something for her too. She was the only person who looked at him like he was normal. Even Adam would hesitate to come near him when Tom was upset or angry. Sam put herself in the way of danger to comfort him. He would never do anything to hurt her, but how could she know that?

Their relationship blossomed and became more and more intense over time. Adam felt left out of the friendship because of the time they were spending alone together, but was too afraid to express his feelings to them about it. One particular night stood out in the memories, Tom was transported to his basement, where he had set everything up for his first date with Sam.

There was romantic French music softly singing from the stereo. He had set up a table for two and made chicken parmesan with spaghetti marinara. His mother had let him light candles to make the mood romantic and had even purchased flowers for him to give Sam, at Tom's request. She would do anything to make her son happy, because of the scene he had to witness with his father. Tom would always remain the most important person in her life.

Tom remembered the moment clearly, when his heart was beating fastest as he opened the front door to see Sam in a beautiful dress. Before now, she had always been dressed in jeans and a t-shirt. The role they played in each other's lives was changing. She was even more beautiful than he had known possible. He remembered the bland taste of the spaghetti that had seemed like the best meal of his life at the time, not because of the food, but because of the company. He remembered the intimate nights of making out on the couch as they let movies play in the background. The first time they said they love each other. It had all been so beautiful. The perfect relationship. Then came the bad.

"You don't care about me anymore," said Adam to Tom, "it used to be the three of us, now you spend all of your time with her. What happened to us? We used to be inseparable. You two never even considered how I would feel about it." Adam was fighting with him about how close Tom had gotten with his sister, and how Tom had pushed him aside in the process.

"Adam, wait," said Tom, "it's not like that."

"You are supposed to be my friend, not hers."

"That's not fair. We can all be friends. There is enough time for everyone. Relationships change. They adapt as we get older. Don't be like this."

Then Tom found himself in a speeding car, driven recklessly by Adam with Sam in the back seat. Their argument still had a long way to go before Adam would be satisfied with the outcome.

"I just want things to be the way they were," said Adam, stepping harder on the gas pedal.

"Adam, stop the car," Sam yelled from the back. "We can talk about this."

"It's okay, Adam, we are both here for you. I never meant for..." Tom was interrupted by the headlights from the other car that were in the periphery of his vision. They crashed head-on. Both drivers had been drinking that night. Tom, once again disoriented in the memories he was experiencing, pulled the bodies from the wreckage. He could have stopped it. Why didn't he do something. Everyone in their car was alive, they found out at the hospital. The doctors were amazed that Tom hadn't suffered any injuries from the accident.

"None of you should have made it out of that car alive," the Doctor said, not yet mentioning that Adam would be in a coma for the rest of his life. Sam directly blamed Tom for what had happened. Subconsciously she wished he could or would do something about it. They fought about it countless times when they had been drinking. He was becoming like his father. Tom was glad he didn't have to relive all those memories in detail. The next thing he remembered, was growing more and more apart from Sam. He saw their final argument, when she had walked in on him with another woman.

"People are just toys," he said, "they all break or wear out eventually. Everything gets old with time."

"I know you don't mean that. You told me you love me," Sam said, fighting back tears.

"You are just another toy," words Tom wished he could take back. He had been so hurt that he shut himself off. He wouldn't let her in, even worse, he pushed her away, as if his feelings were more important than hers. He had been as violent as he could be to her with words.

His mind was completely present this time as he heard the last words she would say to him: "I can tell you don't want me here anymore. I am leaving. Call me if you ever wake up, if you ever want to let me in. The only thing I did wrong was love you. You say you can do anything, but you can't even do that, and it is the most important thing there is. Tell me you don't love me, and I will leave." Tom refused to say anything.

"It is late, I am going to bed. If you want to stay then stay, if not, get out."

"Just tell me you love me," she begged him.

"Get out!" Tom yelled for the last time and threw her out of the house with his mind. It had not been violent, just sudden. He left her standing outside holding the things she had left there in her arms. He could hear her sobbing through the window for the next twenty minutes. He was crying too, but he would never let her know that. That was why he had to get her away from him. To escape. He put his forehead against the door thinking about having her in his arms again as he wished it all away.

Tom remembered that this was the final time he would have his memories erased. He couldn't deal with himself. It hurt too much knowing that he could be so terrible to the only person who would ever accept him for who he was. The only person he ever had such strong feelings for.

His memory flooded back in of the few years he had spent working and living on his own and the empty feeling in his heart, like something had been taken from him. He went on his quest to find what he was missing and ended up meeting the guru who pretended to give him the powers he had always had. Tom now realized that the guru hadn't really done anything. He thought that the powers came from someone else, not that he had grown up with them. The guru was just acting as a gateway to allow his mind to reactivate them after the last complete memory wipe. He was on his own now, with limitless power at his fingertips, and he still didn't want anything or care what happened. Tom was going through his listless existence when he decided that he would spend the rest of his life granting wishes like the guru, so that he could make people happier. He liked the idea of helping people to suffer less.

Chapter 8
Man Who Sold the World

After having spent the time before meeting his guru with nothing, Tom was ready for an ascetic lifestyle. It didn't matter how much he kept around him, his own emptiness would always prevail. He didn't need very much to live on because everything that he could have meant so little to him. There was something bigger that was still out of his reach. Tom had lost his attachments by forgetting his past and future. Nothing mattered to him. He embraced and accepted the present moment as all that there was, but he soon found out that it was harder than he thought to make other people happy. He would learn that most people are only concerned with themselves and the things that they imagined would make them happy. Everybody had an excuse for why they weren't happy and thought that their problems could be solved with one wish.

Tom walked down the street free for the first time in his life. Nothing was weighing him down. It didn't matter anymore, all of it was visible to him. The world was free and clear. Tom wished it could be like this for everyone. Instead of suffering their way through life, people could be free and clear, in charge of their own reality. Everyone was holding on so tightly to the things that were important to them. There was no need. Nothing was important. We lose everything whether we hold on or not. It is a game of understanding. This was the first time Tom found himself floating. These thoughts were not his, but an observation of the author as an interpretation of the emptiness in an egoic nature. Tom himself, felt like he had a clear mind. He was not thinking at all, but simply existing and enjoying it. Everything was perfect, Tom could see it with clear eyes. Some people stared on at him, wishing they could feel that way, sensing that there was something different about him, even though they couldn't see him floating. Others simply continued their existence, involved and wrapped up in their cell phones or where they would go for dinner that night.

Tom saw the universe in a sort of sticky way. Everything that was touched by something else would have a slight wobble to it, even the smallest pressure moved the molecules visibly to Tom. Everything had an impact on everything else. Living things like plants that seem stationary to us were breathing to Tom. He could see them inhale and exhale. There was a visible field around them. It was a whole new sensory experience. While Tom was rubbing the leaves of a plant he had come across, he was interrupted by an older gentleman in a fedora, who was worried about how involved Tom had become with the plant.

"Are you okay, son?" the old man asked him.

"Yes. Everything is so perfect, so beautiful," Tom replied dreamily.

"Ah, I see. I wish I had learned that twenty years ago. Life would have been a lot easier."

"Is that your wish, sir? I can make it come true for you."

"Well, no, it was more small talk. You know how us old folks are. I wouldn't trade my experiences for anything."

"What would you wish for?" Tom asked.

"Me? I never thought about it. That's one of the reason's I am such a happy person. If you spend all of your time wishing, wondering, and thinking about what could be, you would miss what is there right in front of you."

"I know what you mean. So you wouldn't wish for anything?" Tom asked.

"I have had a long and full life. There is nothing I haven't had up until now that I can't live without."

"You could live forever, or another lifetime at least."

"Another one! Ha. This one has already been so much. Even if that were possible, why would I want to keep living and watch my loved ones grow older and die?"

"That's a good point. Then there is nothing I can do for you to repay your kindness."

"Just paying attention to me is more than enough. You wouldn't believe how many people walk by me without giving me the time of day. It is hard when you are older. People don't take you seriously and don't want to spend any time with you. They are missing out on all the life lessons that they will learn when they are older."

"I think I know what I can do for you then," Tom smiled, "have a beautiful day."

"You do the same," said the older man slowly walking away to his next destination. Tom knew the man would be going to his favorite Sunday evening hang out. The man liked to sit by the window and talk to people as they came in and left the coffee shop by the park. As he was walking there, the old man would be interrupted by his grandson, who had a school project to do and wanted to hear all about his grandfather's life. Something told Tom that this would only be the first time somebody important to the man would want to spend time with him before he died in his sleep three years from now. After all, isn't that what most of us want, to have loved ones spend time with us? The old man's existence had been perfect to Tom. Tom wanted to live the same way, knowing what is important and not wanting to change anything.

The thought was interrupted by a homeless man asking for change.

"What is it you really want?" Tom asked him.

"Just a few bucks, mister, I'm not asking for much."

"You can have anything you want, just name it."

"Okay, how about a hundred?" The homeless man said to him, thinking it was a far fetch, but wanting to take advantage of the offer. Tom smiled. This would be one of the first times when helping people would cause suffering. He pulled a brand new crisp one-hundred dollar bill from his pocket and handed it to the man.

The man was exhilarated at first, he could hardly believe his luck. "Gee, thanks mister, God bless you!" said the homeless man. It seemed like a nice thing to do. After all, it was what the man had asked for, but every day after that the homeless man would wonder how much more money he could have asked for. What he could have gotten became more important to him than the hundred he did receive. His mind made the wish into a curse, never happy with what had happened, but instead obsessing over what could have been. On top of that, no one would ever seem as generous. The few dollars he received from others would seem like an insult to him after he had seen the potential for more.

With his vision of the beyond, Tom saw one possible timeline where people surrounded him begging for money as a newscaster told the incredible story of a man parting with his wealth to help the less fortunate. This wish business would be harder than he thought. A lot of people didn't really know what they wanted. Most of them thought they did, but it was always something short-term, momentary thinking. No one wanted anything lasting and meaningful. Tom understood why his guru was in such a remote location. Only people who were ready would be able to reach him. That was what he needed to do. If people are willing to seek you out, they have spent considerably more time thinking about what it is that they want to see change in their life. They would have to make a serious effort to prove they could handle their wish wisely. People like Tom. They are searching and searching for something but they don't quite know what it is. Their wish should be to find it. To find fulfillment, either in what they have or what they are going after.

"So be it," Tom said to himself, "only those who are ready will be able to find me." Tom zapped himself out of there into a beautiful temple in the mountains. This would give him time to enjoy his new peace of mind as well. It was such a remote location, only those who truly sought would be able to find it.

Tom was not alone at the temple. It had already been occupied by a group of monks, who were more than generous enough to allow him to stay, as long as he helped out with the work that needed to be done. Tom could complete all of the work in the blink of an eye, but he used it to occupy his time meditatively. Tom was learning the ways of the monks. It was a peaceful, solitary lifestyle of quiet contemplation and meditation. It was very simple, but very beautiful. When they were hungry they would eat, and when they were tired they would sleep. He had fun joking around with the other monks in simple, child-like ways, such as hitting each other in the rear with the broom while they swept. In a way, it helped remind all of them to be aware instead of wrapped up in their minds. Everything was new and exciting. There was no anger, greed, or want. Everything seemed perfect.

Tom didn't know it, but the monks had run out of money, and the local government was trying to force them out. On the final day, a bill collector came to the temple. A crowd gathered as the head monk, Seefu, was sent out to talk to the bill collector. Many of the monks had taken a vow of silence, and it was the duty of the head monk to discuss outside business with anybody who came to the temple for worldly reasons.

"If we don't receive payment in ten days, we will forcibly evict the premises," said the bill collector, handing him a notice. Seefu read the letter with great anguish in his face. This was the first time Tom had seen him so greatly disturbed.

"Please. We are a poor and simple people. We do not have a lot of money, but what we don't have in money we make up for in spirit. Our temple has been here long before your government moved in. You must respect our ability to live peacefully alongside your culture."

"I am just here to deliver the notice. I have no say in it," said the bill collector, clearly irritated by their plight.

"We will give what we can, but this amount is three times more than what we make in a year! It is not possible for us to pay this. Your government knows that!"

"Then you know where we stand. You have ten days to pay or leave."

Tom snapped his fingers to remedy the situation. One of the other monks ran out of the temple to Seefu with a letter in his hand. The monk was so very excited, he broke his twenty year vow of silence at this point to share the good news.

"Seefu! Seefu! You have to see this!" said the monk.

"Gyan-tsen! You are speaking! Remember your vow."

"I am sorry, Seefu, but you have to read this, we're saved!" The monk, or Gyan-tsen as they knew him, gave Seefu the letter. It was carefully read over, then even he, the great master, threw up his hands in excitement. He quickly regained his poise and again addressed the bill collector, as well as the rest of the onlookers.

"It seems that thanks to an anonymous donation, we will be able to pay our bills, and stay in the temple. Indefinitely."

It was now the bill collector's turn to frown. The town had known all along that the temple wouldn't be able to pay such an outrageous sum of money. They just wanted to get them out of there so they could control the whole city.

"Gyan-tsen, go to the bank with this man and take out the necessary funds from our account," said Seefu. Gyan-tsen couldn't go fast enough.

As the crowd dispersed and things at the temple calmed down, Seefu spoke offhand to Tom. "We would have found a way to survive," he said, "everything happens as it was meant to."

A Struggle of Ego

Chapter 9
Bring Me Fire!

Tom didn't know how exactly it had happened, but the universe found a way to communicate the need for people to find Tom and ask him for things. It was not a big deal at first. A person here or there would come and ask for his blessing and other simple things. They would ask for their kids to pass tests they had been studying for, to get jobs they were applying for, and promotions they had been waiting for. Tom assured all of them that what was best would happen and sent them on their way.

It quickly escalated out of control. There was a line of people hundreds deep every day, all wanting him to solve their problems. With this multitude of people, came unsavory characters alongside the dedicated believers. People who wanted things for their own benefit, sometimes at the expense of others. The purity of the people who were coming for his blessing was fading. Even some of the early followers were begging him for things they didn't need, not ready to surrender their lives to a higher power. With this multitude of people came large donations for the temple, but it had disrupted the peace of the mountain. Finally, Seefu came to Tom, who knew exactly what was going to happen.

"I can see you are a very good person, Tom, you are trying your best to help people, but you must know that people need to find help from within themselves, not from the instant-gratification of the wishes you grant," said the monk.

65

"I just want to help people. Why is it so much harder than it has to be? Nobody is ever happy with what they get."

"That is the nature of people. The mind keeps them disquieted so that they will keep striving for more. If they were happy the way they are, they would stop creating and going on in life. The struggle of existence provides greater motivation than having things handed to us."

"But look how peaceful it is here," Tom replied.

"It is peaceful, but it is also still. Without their desires, people would not be able to be part of the society that they have created. They need to keep building so they feel like they have purpose. You and I know that is not important, but they are still young minds that have not been freed from their conditioning. Fulfill one desire and ten will take its place. Everything you give creates a bigger hole in their lives to balance it out."

"I see. All along it has been me who is holding on to something. I must move through life without trying to change lives," Tom said, seeing how his mission was a lost cause, and even worse, just another attachment.

"That is right. Work only on yourself. If the universe wants you to help others, it will give you the opportunity. You cannot force it on anyone. Thank you for helping to save our temple, and I know you will grant us respect by returning to where you are meant to be."

"Yes, Seefu. I know I have to leave." Tom bowed to the great master and disappeared from the room. His monk robes changed back into his everyday clothing as he was back home. Tom spent the next few days getting everything in order. He purchased a house and car, deciding he would live there for as long as he was meant to. Tom hadn't needed to buy anything, but the process was entertaining.

Having spent so much time away from society, these little social conventions were enjoyable to him. A short time later, Tom decided he would go to the store and see all of the new things he had missed. He got into his car and flew away to where he would meet Sam for the first time, once again.

Tom woke up in his bedroom after having everything restored. The memories were all connected together now in logical order. Some of the later memories in the temple had never been erased for Tom, but he wanted me to include them in that order, so the audience would have an idea of who he had been and what he had done after losing his memories. Tom thought it reflected poorly only to show the bad things instead of the good he tried to accomplish.

So there he was, back at home, with his memories restored. Tom now knew exactly why Sam was mad at him. He was hesitant as to what to do next. There were so many choices and he couldn't see the outcomes. He wanted to spend the rest of his life with Sam. Had she spent all of those years studying law enforcement just to find his guru? He wasn't sure if it was better or worse now than it had been before he met her in the store.

Tom got up out of bed and noticed something strange. There was a smell. Something unpleasant. It would not be overpowering to most, but Tom, who hadn't experienced this in so long, had forgotten what it was like. He was smelling himself. His body. Tom hadn't had an unpleasant odor since the day he was given his power. He normally had a scent similar to that of a temple, burning incense and flowers. It was… normal. Why was this happening? Tom waved his hand over his own body expecting the smell to dissipate, but nothing happened. John had been right. The memories were making him attached. He cared about the outcome of his life once again, and wanted to spend his time with Sam. He snapped his fingers to change his outfit. Nothing happened. Tom was getting irritated. He had been gliding through his life before and now he couldn't even manifest a new outfit.

He closed his eyes and tried to see, to connect with the stream of existence that was all around, where he could normally see everything. There was just blackness. Tom was experiencing duality. He was separated from the whole once again. Tom imagined the dramatic music that should be playing, were this ever to be made into a movie, but couldn't hear it out loud the way he used to. He no longer knew what the Latin words meant. Dies irae, dies illa, solvet saeclum in favilla. It was so weird! Tom felt his body in a different way. Things were achy and tight. Very limited. His vision was back to being his own vision instead of the infinite universe. Was this the price for being with Sam? They weren't even together yet. He had to do something. Take the memories away again? No. He needed them. The memories made him who he was. Tom was getting lost in his own mind. What if she didn't like him like this? He had always had the upper hand with everyone else, and now he was on a level playing field.

Chapter 10
Enkindling

In this panicked state of mind, Tom decided the best thing to do was to call for help. He grabbed his cell phone and stared at it blankly. Tom had never really used his phone, but simply made it carry out his will. There were all kinds of things on the screen and he had no idea where to start. After a while of fumbling around with it, Tom found the phone keypad and entered the number that was still written on the piece of paper in his pocket. It was practically a miracle that it was still there. The universe had allowed it. He dialed the number and pressed call. It rang. The same brrr, brrr, brrr, that readers will remember from the beginning of the story. Tom was clenching his teeth in a different sort of anticipation than last time.

Sam answered the phone, "Hello?"

"Sam, it's Tom, I need your help, something has happened," said Tom.

"What? Tom? What did you do? I have never heard you like this before."

"You have to help me, I smell."

"Really? You had me worried. That's what soap is for, Tom."

"You're not getting it, have you ever known me to smell?"

She took a moment to think about it. "I don't know," she replied.

"Think about it. Seriously. I have never smelled before."

"So go take a shower." It still wasn't registering.

"Sam. I lost my powers," he said.

...

"Did you hear me?" Tom asked.

"You read the letter? It woke up the memories..." she said.

"Yes."

"And what do you think about it?"

"It's horrible. All of it. I hate myself. I love you. What else is there to say?"

"You are clearly not in the right state of mind. I don't know if I should take any of that as a compliment or hang up on you."

"Sam! Please. You have to help me get the powers back."

"I don't know. What if it's better this way? Maybe you and I can be happy together. Maybe we can have a normal life now."

"That is what I want. I know. I'm sorry for acting this way, it is just so different to have it one minute and nothing the next."

"I'll be able to stop by tonight. Until then, just do things like a normal person. Take a shower, put on deodorant, have something to eat."

"What time will you..." Tom didn't finish his sentence.

"What? Be there?" she asked.

"Nothing, I just thought I saw something. When do you think you'll make it?" There had been something in the side of Tom's vision. It felt like someone had been in the room with him. There was a tingling sensation up his spine and a slight chill that made him shudder. There was nothing there when he looked.

"It probably won't be until after six," Sam said.

"Okay. Thank you," Tom replied, still a bit shaken up from thinking he saw something.

They both disconnected from the phone conversation. Sam had a bigger smile than she would admit as she went back to work and Tom was left sitting on the edge of his bed letting it all sink in.

Tom thought to himself about all of the things he could no longer do. He was making himself feel bad until he remembered the reason he had made this choice. He would be able to spend the rest of his life with Sam. That was worth it. A big grin unintentionally found it's home on his face. She was coming! And he smelled. Tom decided to listen to her advice and take a shower.

Tom went into the bathroom, pulled back the shower curtain. There was a tub. Good. Tom hadn't actually seen it before now. He bought the house knowing he could change any part of it he didn't like, but now it was beneficial that the bathroom had a shower. He turned the knob for the water. After a rattling noise in the wall and a bit of dirty water, there was fresh, clean water running from the tap. He put his hand under it, feeling how the water ran through his fingers. It was beautiful. He adjusted the temperature to make it nice and hot, then pulled the plug so the water would go through the showerhead instead of the lower faucet. Tom didn't know if these were the right words but assumed people would be able to figure out what he was doing.

He took off his clothes and got in the shower. It was heavenly. Warm water flowing all over his body, it was incredible. Tom had lost a lot of the simple pleasures of life, and this was one of them. He put his head back and let the water rush down his body enjoying the sensation. It felt like the energy he had flowing through him before. The cascade of being surrounded by energy. Tom closed his eyes and moaned. It was taking him away from his problems and worries. Tom's mind was clear while he was in the shower. If he looked outside of the curtain, he would have noticed some of the objects floating, but it was too enjoyable for distraction. The ingenuity of it held him in this state of euphoria. That is one of the secrets to life. Live as if everything is new and exciting. Let yourself be taken away into that world of surprise and delight.

After spending entirely too much time in the shower, Tom's skin was getting pruney and he decided that he would have to carry on with his life instead of living in this aquatic paradise. He grabbed one of the decorative towels off of the towel bar and dried himself off. He went in to the bedroom and opened the closet. There was nothing in it.

"Huh," Tom said, "I guess I will have to go clothes-shopping." He opened up his dresser drawers, still nothing.

"Well, when you have one outfit, you wear it," Tom said, putting on the clothes he had taken off before getting in the shower. It didn't feel quite as clean and new as a fresh pair would have, but what else could he do?

Time felt so long. He was waiting for Sam to come. There was no food in the fridge... why did he even have a refrigerator? It was decorative. That's what normal people had, so that's what his house had. He did manage to make a decent pot of coffee. Even with his powers, Tom would take the time to make his own coffee. It was a habitual ritual that gave him comfort.

So he sat on his porch sipping his coffee with a strange pain in his stomach that would later be identified as hunger. The little nuances of life had gone over his head, but now he was faced with them as any normal person would be. What time was it? He usually knew without looking. He had seen that his phone had the time on it the last time he looked at it. Tom pulled out his phone and pressed one of the buttons. Five-thirty. She should be here in half an hour. Tom took another sip of his coffee. What was he going to do? There was no Einstein, and no Buddha to give him ideas or advice. There was an overwhelming feeling of aloneness that Tom had not been privy to up until now. Something different about not knowing what else is out there. It had an empty, sad feeling to it that Tom couldn't describe. Things mattered more to him now. Sam being in his life felt like a weight upon his heart, it made his chest heavy.

For the first time Tom felt like he could lose her. Even when she was gone, he hadn't felt this way. Helpless. How did people carry on through life like this? A book would be nice. Was he trying to be distracted? Occupied? Time seemed to need filling now, instead of being a blessing unto itself. It wasn't until six forty-five that Sam finally pulled her car up in front of his house. It literally felt like forever. He had been sitting there, waiting, nothing happening, drinking coffee. He was shaking at this point from the lack of food and the caffeine from the amount of coffee he had been drinking, not realizing that two cups is plenty for a normal person. Tom had been immune to its effects up to this point. He was beginning to realize why people liked it so much. He thought it was just because of the luxury and finesse. The care that could be put into it had always been alluring to him, not the buzz. Now his stomach hurt.

"Do you want some coffee?" Tom asked her as she walked up the path.

"Is that all you've been drinking?" she asked him.

"There is no food in the house. I can see why people like coffee, it feels amazing."

"You need to eat something. Let's go get dinner," Sam said.

"Our first date," Tom said looking hopefully at her.

"Whoa, slow down there, kiddo."

"What do you mean? I got my memories back so we could be together. What about last time when we went out?"

"Last time was different, you didn't know anything about us. It was light and fun. Now that you remember everything, there is a lot between us. It is not something we can just speed by, we have to talk about it and work through it."

"But, it was all an accident. I'm not the person who did those things and made the wrong choices. Up until recently I didn't even know he existed in the first place. I am still the good person I was yesterday, not some monster I forgot about."

"But *it did happen*. It happened to me. It happened to both of us. Part of you is always going to be that person. I can't act like it didn't hurt the way it did."

"That's not fair. I'm not that person. I am only the person I am right now, not some collection of memories. I gave up everything so that we could be together," Tom said, his ego crushed.

"And we will be. It just can't happen overnight, that's all. I love you, but it's going to take time before I can trust you again. I need to feel comfortable before I can open myself back up to you. It hurt so much."

"But I did this to myself for you. I want us to be together. There is nothing but love. I want to spend the rest of my life with you. I have never been more open and vulnerable. Getting my memories back made me realize that I need you in my life, no matter what the price, and that means opening up to you. I want to be vulnerable with you."

"I know, and I appreciate that, but it's not so simple that it can just be turned on or off, it is a mutual understanding. I need time to open back up to you. Come on, let's go get dinner," Sam said.

Dinner carried on in a similar manner. They had switched places. That is what Sam had wished for. She wanted him to understand what it was like for everyone else around him. Tom was finding out that it was not as glamorous as he had imagined it would be. It wasn't a pleasure for everyone just to be in his presence. He wasn't the greatest thing since sliced bread. He was just another person. Worst of all, Sam wasn't ready to accept her love for him, or open up to it. Getting hurt will do that to a person. One can only hope they realize it before they are out of time.

Tom loved the dinner. The dinner itself, not the way the conversation went between him and Sam. The food tasted new to him. Up until now food had just been food. Now it was life sustaining and the taste had flooded his mouth as if it were the first time he had really eaten. It was unfortunate that Sam couldn't see where he was coming from. They were both in different places. The conversation went something like this.

"This soup is incredible," Tom said to her.

"I'm sure it's not that good," She replied.

"I'm really enjoying it. Everything is so amazing."

"Come on, it's just soup."

"I never knew soup was so good."

"Enough about the soup."

"Have you eaten here before?"

"You mean, have I ever been here on a date?" Sam asked.

"No, that's not what I mean at all. I just wondered if you had been here before," Tom said.

"I have been here, we both have, don't you remember anything?"

"I did just get my memories back, some of it is still fuzzy. I guess I have a lot on my mind right now."

"So what are you going to do now that you are a normal person again?"

"I hadn't thought past being with you," Tom said.

"Awe." Sam said, still confusing awe with aww. That had always bothered him when they texted. Though he had assumed that she was expressing that he was sweet, not that she was surprised. Maybe it was both, that she was surprised he was sweet. The thought of it was funny to Tom.

"That is all I ever really wanted," Tom said.

"You'll have to do something to make money. What do you want to do with yourself?"

"I don't really want to work. It has always felt like such a chore. Everyone wants something of you instead of letting you live life or do things the way you want."

"You have to work. That's how you can afford all of the nice things you have in your life."

"I don't need anything. I am happy with just you."

"Awe, baby, I know you just want to be with me, but it is important that we make money and have something to live on."

A very passive-aggressive night left Tom wanting for something more. It wasn't the love he remembered. The illusion of what had been was broken and all that was left was the current point of view. Things couldn't just go back to the way they were without putting anything into it. It might never happen. What if she never let him in? Tom was starting to regret his decision. He should have left well-enough alone, but the illusion of the love was so alluring. He did want to be with Sam, but not this Sam, the Sam who he had known when he was younger. The girl who was carefree and thought the world of him. The Sam that was created by his mind, not the real Sam and who she was now.

This girl was closed-off and complicated. He didn't want to have to work for love, it was already beaming so brightly in him, the hope and idea of it. His heart hurt knowing this wasn't going to be the relationship he wanted. What had he expected? Things can never go back to the way they were. It was part of the egoic mind. Always glorifying the past and the future, leaving out the present moment. It wasn't worth it. His present moment was suffering. There was no idea of what could be one day, just the pain he was feeling now. Tom wanted out of these new hurtful feelings, but was left with no powers to escape from them. So he did the next best thing, that which all of us do. He tried to get away from himself.

Tom found himself at the busiest nightclub in town taking drink after drink. He hated everyone and everything around him. All of them. It was just his own projection, just as it had been all along tonight. Nothing was real, but now Tom had the horrible luxury of understanding what it means when the mind creates all of it around you. Everything meant something, the way people moved or walked by, the music, the environment. His mind was flooded with interpretations of everything and it was devastating. Everyone projects their own idea of what is going on and what it means, and Tom was a part of it now.

His mind was not silent. His emotion's and feeling's were being put out toward the world and it could be seen a mile away. He couldn't let go so he kept drinking, hoping that there would at least be solace in sleep or a drunken stupor.

It was a busy night. Plenty of things to see, people to watch. Tom was more interested in forgetting his problems than dealing with them, but spent most of the night suffering from the thoughts he was having. They were strong. He wasn't used to fighting with his mind over what became the present moment. Everything had always felt perfect, and now there was turmoil. He wouldn't be able to do anything.

There was no way he would go back to work, and there wasn't anything he was particularly interested in. That is how he felt, at least. Life had been easy for the last few years and he had lost everything. Nothing could convince him that he even had Sam. She made it quite clear that she needed time, but Tom didn't have the ability to give it to her. He needed love and support as he went through this major change in his life, but he was left to deal with it alone.

"Boy, you sure have let yourself go." There was a man in a suit sitting next to him at the bar. He was talking to Tom. Tom swung his head up with an irritated expression on his face to look at the man, but when he saw him, he didn't know who this person was. That was another thing Tom had lost, being able to know people without knowing them.

"Do I know you?" Tom asked him, questioning why this man was interrupting his stewing.

"I wouldn't be very good at my job if you did," said the man. "It was wrong of her to let you out without asking her superiors."

"You mean Sam? You work for them?"

"You could say that. I am not at liberty to discuss my position with the company. I came here to talk to you because it seems you don't have any value to us now. Someone took the juice out of your cannon, huh?" Tom wasn't in love with that terrible metaphor. What kind of a cannon runs on juice? An orange cannon? It had to be some kind of juice canon, right? Tom didn't like that people called fuel juice. Nobody drinks gasoline or electricity, so stop using the same words interchangeably, he thought to himself.

"Is there something I can help you with?" Tom finally asked, letting go of his distaste for the phrase about the juice cannon.

"Well, this is the first time I have been able to get close enough to talk to you, and it seems like it would have been a waste not to take advantage of this unique opportunity. To think, we were worried you would blow our heads up or make us forget who we are. Now you can't even go on a date like a normal person." How long had they been watching him? How much did they know? Tom hadn't thought about this and it was too late to gain any intel on it because he had no ability to do so.

"Sam is our asset," continued the man, "I have you to thank for that, she has been a valuable part of the team, but that was because of her connection with you. I doubt she would have gotten as far as she did if you two didn't know each other. It's weird you know, half the time it seems like she really cares about you, than the other half she just wants to take you down. I was waiting for the day she would stop talking about your powers and what you could do with them, but never thought it would happen. She finally found a way to make you vulnerable, and you did it to yourself. Willingly, no less. What dedication for the job."

"I know the whole story. What is it I can do for you?" Tom asked, irritated with what the man was saying. This guy was pushing his buttons and he knew it. It is a good thing he didn't have his powers anymore, for this man's sake.

"Hey, we're just talking," the man said, throwing up his hands innocently, "it seems we have friends in common. I just wanted you to know that your actions have never gone unnoticed. If you ever thought about doing something stupid, remember that we have Sam. She is working for us, and somehow I feel like it would bother you if anything ever happened to her."

"It doesn't matter anymore. None of it does. I *don't* have my powers and it doesn't seem like things are going well with Sam and I."

"That's not the impression I got from her. I thought you two finally had a chance to be together," said the man in the suit.

"She only knows what she sees. I only know what I see."

"You don't think it's going to work out?"

"Does that put her at risk?" Tom asked.

"Her, at risk? No. Not even her job. We don't care about you anymore and she is a good agent. As far as I'm concerned, as long as she is doing her job diligently, that is all that matters. I can't vouch for anything that happens in the field, but that is one of the risks of the job, right?"

"Will you keep her safe for me?" Tom asked, grasping at straws, as if he had any sway over this man.

"For you? Ha. I don't know. I do my best to protect all of our assets. You don't seem like you have much going on in your life, why do you ask? Are you planning on doing something stupid?"

"Planning on it. Yeah, but not what you think. Nobody is at risk, but me."

"And Sam?"

"Only because she loves me."

"It would be nice to stop seeing your files pop up on my desk, but I never said that. You know they wanted to have you locked up again, even though you can't do anything? I told them not to waste the cell. I can't believe you gave up all that power for her. Such a cliché my man, giving up everything for a woman." The man in the suit was rubbing Tom's back playfully, but it was only serving to make him more angry.

"I'm starting to feel that way too. I gave up my whole world for a dream, a memory, a faded vision of something that I am not finding in the real world."

"Love comes from within. Not from without, but I didn't come here to be your guidance counselor. I just wanted you to know that no good deed goes unpunished, but you seem to already know that."

"It never pays to be selfish. I didn't do it because I love her, I did it because I wanted that person back. I wanted who she was, the only person who loved me for who I am, not the person she is now. I can't stand the way she looked at me, like she was afraid of what I would do."

"Do you mind telling me what it is you plan on doing about it? I promise I won't tell Sam," said the man in the suit, as if he was someone worth trusting, if only for keeping him out of prison.

"Right now I just want to get away from this. I don't know how to deal with it. It is something I can't figure out. Not just having lost my powers, but now feeling completely disillusioned with the love I imagined. It doesn't feel like it's there at all," Tom said.

"Well, I support anything that gets you out of my jurisdiction. I'm tired of your files piling up on my desk and being held responsible for your actions."

"They hold you responsible for me? That doesn't seem fair."

"That's what I keep telling them. Do me a favor. If you ever get your powers back, make it so I never have to hear anything about it."

"Deal. Any idea how I would do that?"

"Me? Ha! If I knew that I would be in Florida on the beach, sipping an island drink that has an umbrella and an abundance of tropical fruit. You know how hard it is to get a vacation for a job like mine? I have you to thank for that. You'll have to forgive me if I'm not exactly rooting for you to get your powers, when it means I'll have to go back to watching you all day." The man in the suit smirked and walked away. He had said what he came to say.

Tom turned around on his bar stool to see if there was anyone else he could talk to. Someone who could help him forget. He didn't see anybody that he was interested in talking to or taking home, so he made his way toward the exit, but he was stopped. An interesting man with some kind of electronic device on his arm stepped in front of him. Tom looked at the man with disdain, wondering what he wanted from him.

"Name's Shaun," said the man, "you look like something is missing from your life. There was something big I missed too. Felt like we might be kindred spirits."

What kind of accent was this? The man sounded like he was pretending to be Australian or something, but who was Tom to judge in this state of mind?

A moment of clarity, "I just need to get home and sleep. Nothing is making me feel better," Tom said.

"Ah, that's your problem right there. Trying to get away from yourself. Everything comes from within, but when what you want isn't coming, there is something for that. Here," Shaun said handing him a sugar cube.

"What is this?"

"It's a window. Eat it now. Should be working by the time you get home." In his drunken stupor, Tom took candy from the stranger and headed out of the bar. He didn't notice that no one else in the bar could see Shaun. He had come from somewhere far away to help Tom in his search.

Chapter 11
The Window

The walk home was a good opportunity for him to get some fresh air. It was a mile and a half walk that felt like forever to someone under the influence. Especially traveling it alone. The world was spinning slightly as he looked around at the buildings that were still lit up, shining their lights into the darkness. The path was not well-lit, but Tom liked the dark. The lights were hurting his eyes. Everything seemed brighter than normal. The candy was working fast because of the amount he had drank. Tom could see quite far in the dark. There was a squirrel sitting up in a tree. Some kind of animal ran by in the distance, maybe it was a dog, maybe a fox. He was becoming a predator as his mind finally started to feel still. When he got inside his house, he left the lights off. He could see everything just fine without them. His stomach was hurting in a strange way that he had never felt before. It was not hunger, but a hot feeling like something was coming to life inside of him. His breath was heavy and felt like he was breathing through another dimension.

Tom was light-headed, but not just from the alcohol. He felt everything around him through his own beating heart. Everything was pulsing, in a way that was similar to when he had powers, but not quite there. He could see a dim light around his arms and body when he looked down. Tom didn't have the control or awareness that permeated his existence while controlling the universe this time. It felt similar, but like he was forcing his way into something he wasn't meant to experience. He sat on his couch cross-legged and rocked back and forth slightly to his own beating heart, while experiencing this new sensation. He waved his hand in front of his eyes and saw it as if in slow motion, images of his hand followed as it moved in front of him. There were little things moving around in the dark, but they would disappear when he tried to focus on them. He kept seeing things out of the corner of his eye, but nothing would be there if he turned on the lights. Everything was moving. That's what it looked like to him, at least. Whose eyes was he seeing through?

Tom started to go deeper into whatever it was Shaun had given him. He spoke out loud to hear his voice, because to him it sounded as if he were speaking in a large auditorium. His voice echoed, sounding like it was coming from very far away. His senses had slowed down. Tom was feeling like he used to, as if he could control things again, but it was just a vision of it, not a reality. He was trying to hold on to it when what he saw out of the corner of his eye stepped out fully into his vision.

A man walked across the room and sat down in an easy chair. Tom was frightened at first, realizing that it was himself. The man was Tom. He could feel it, he was sitting there across from himself. Who was sitting on the couch then if that was him? The lack of continuity relaxed his thoughts from the initial fear. The figure in the chair stared at Tom with a wider than life grin.

'If that's me over there, who is me over here?' Tom asked himself. The figure did not speak. It just stared at him with big wide eyes, grinning. Tom made noises, still fascinated by how his voice sounded, trying in some way to see if this other version of him would react. Tom was still seeing everything else moving, and it was hard for him to focus on any one thing because of the distortion. He tried to see what this version of himself was trying to tell him. There didn't seem to be any obvious meaning. The figure just sat there staring at him smiling wider and wider. Tom stared back. It was getting creepy for him.

Tom got up and left the room, the figure in the chair watching him the whole time. He was hoping that the figure would stay in the living room if he left. He stood outside of the room with his back against the wall breathing hard, following his breath and wishing the figure away.

When Tom reached the bedroom, the figure was already standing there by his bed waiting. He wouldn't be able to lie in his bed for some time without thinking of this man looming over him now. Tom sighed and went back to the living room. There was no getting away. At least the figure wouldn't be standing over him in the living room.

"Stop staring at me!" Tom finally shouted at this other self he was seeing.

In response, he heard his own voice speaking aloud, but neither of them were opening their mouths.

"Don't you want to get your powers back?"

"Of course I do," said Tom, "I know that," not sure if his mouth was moving either as he spoke.

"Then you already know how to do it, don't you?"

"I suppose you'll tell me how?"

"You have to find him... the guru. He can give them back to you."

"Where can I find him?"

"Not where, how."

"Who is the last person that you know to have seen him?"

"Sam."

"Bingo. She knows where he was last. She can lead you to him."

"Why would she want to? She is the reason my powers were taken away. That was her wish, and she is the one who gave me back the memories. She didn't force them on me, but it's like giving someone a loaded gun and not telling them it's dangerous. I don't think she wants me to have them."

"Then you know that you can't make it sound like you are trying to get them back. Just show interest in her story. Everyone wants to talk about how amazing it is to be around the guru, even you."

It sounded like a good idea. It was the only plan there was at this point beside living like this in misery. The figure didn't go away even though it seemed their conversation had concluded.

"You're just going to sit there, huh?" Tom asked him. There was no reply. He was ready for this to end. It had been hours and it was still affecting him. Everything was still moving and pulsing. He was fidgeting trying to find a comfortable position, but every five minutes he would have to move again. He went from room to room, the figure standing in the shadows around him the whole time. Tom's legs were gone. The feeling in them, I mean. His being seemed to be in the top half of his body. He floated along from room to room forgetting that he ever had legs to take him places. Everything was taking forever. Time had a quality of stillness that stretched it out while Tom was under the effects of whatever it was he had taken. He should have known better, but he had been drinking and wanting to get away. Tom spent eternities in his thoughts, going from one place to the next, all things he would forget when he woke up the next morning. It was good that he didn't have his powers at this point, he wasn't sure what he would do with them, or if they would do things on their own. Maybe it wouldn't have an effect on him at all. Tom's brain was being rewired, pathways were opening that hadn't been used for a long time. He was remembering things and places, events in his life that he had forgotten about. The memories he had gotten back directly from the letter were just surface memories. There was more hidden deeper.

Tom found himself a young child again talking to a psychologist about what had happened with his father, they made it sound like this was what caused him to act out in school. The psychologist was one of those typical middle-aged men who was balding. He wore a smoking jacket and fancy shoes. While the patient talked to him from a fancy leather couch, he took notes on his legal pad of anything that resembled an association to his psychological training. He would never be able to see Tom using his powers, even if he wanted to. If you go to a psychologist when you are sane, you will come out crazy. They will give you a condition to believe is the cause of your suffering. If you don't have your own neurosis, they will create one for you to hold on to so they can be right and continue to keep you as a patient. It is not intentional, it is what they are trained to do.

Tom sat on the couch as Doctor Fletcher encouraged him to open up about what had happened at school that day.

"I guess I just lost control," Tom said, "people like to push and then they're surprised when I fight back. I don't know why adults expect me to sit there and take it. I shouldn't be at fault for not putting up with their garbage."

"Do you think there was a better way to deal with the situation?" asked the doctor.

"Better? Not in the moment. Adults always think they can be there to make sure everyone is okay, but they don't know how kids are. They don't do it in front of the adults because they know they would get in trouble. They just keep pushing and pushing. If I go tell on them that makes me the bad guy and it is even worse. What would you do if someone was consistently rude to you?"

"I would avoid them, but this is not about me. Tom, you know they are just kids being kids. You can ignore them."

"Try ignoring the next guy who pushes you into a wall. They're lucky they can still breathe after how they treat kids like Adam. They just don't learn."

"Have you considered that they are acting out because of their own insecurities? A lot of these kids don't have the home life that you do. They *still* have parents who argue and abuse them."

"Are you saying I'm better off because my dad is dead?"

"No, you misunderstand me, Tom. I'm saying that you don't always know why kids are being mean. Most of the time it is not about you, it is about them and what they are going through."

"It doesn't make any sense. Just because they are going through things they have to hurt other people? Even if it is true, knowing that doesn't make it any easier to deal with. I don't care why it is happening, I won't put up with it happening to me or my friends. Someone has to stand up for the little guy. My dad was the same way. He thought he could push us around."

"I understand what you are saying, but you have to be the bigger man. Your dad has been gone for a long time, and you can't live your life based on this example."

"Why should I? Because I'll get in trouble?" Tom asked.

"No, you know as well as I do that you are not like them. You are stronger than them. If they knew you as well as I do, they would be a lot nicer. You should ask them why they feel the need to be the way they are. There is one more test I need for you to complete before I can give you a full diagnosis. Don't worry. This is an easy one. Just write down the first six numbers that come to your mind." Tom did as he was instructed.

"So what does it mean?"

"I'll let you know at your next appointment. Until then, do me a favor and do your best to ignore these kids. They have problems of their own they are trying to deal with and they need your sympathy."

"I'll try, but I can't make any promises. If there is one thing I know, it is that you can't let people push you around."

A few days later after school, Tom found himself in the same situation. He learned that Adam had been stuck in one of the lockers. This information did not please him one bit. Tom found the locker and opened it without the combination.

"Are you all right?" Tom asked him.

"I think so," said Adam, "thanks for coming to get me out of here."

"Who did this to you?"

"It was that bully, Josh, again. I don't know why they won't just leave me alone." This was the last straw.

"Well, we'll see what he has to say about it."

"It's okay Tom, I'm not hurt. We can just ignore it like the adults keep telling us to," Adam said.

"No, it's not okay. There is no justice in it. People can't treat others like this and expect to get away with it."

"They are just going to make it worse for me if you confront them," Adam said in protest. Tom wouldn't listen. In a second, they found themselves outside of Josh's house ringing the doorbell. A middle aged woman opened the door.

"Can I help you boys?" she asked them.

"We're Josh's friends. Can you send him out to talk to us?" Tom asked her.

"Of course, why don't you come on in? Friends of Josh are always welcome." They did. Josh's mother was very nice. She offered them freshly-baked cookies she had baked and called Josh to come down. Josh was very rude to her.

"What do you want? I'm in the middle of a game," Josh yelled from upstairs.

"There are some friends of yours here to see you."

"Friends? Who?"

"Come and see them, they are waiting," his mother said.

"Ughhh," Josh stormed down stairs into the living room where they were waiting for him.

"You? What are you two doing in my house?" Josh demanded of them.

"We shouldn't be here," Adam said to Tom.

"No. Josh, do you know who I am?" Tom asked him.

"I know that you're both losers. Why are you in my house?"

"Is it true that you locked Adam in a locker today?"

"Yeah, it was hilarious. You should have seen his face." As if that made any sense. How could you see his face if he was locked in a locker?

"Some of us don't find that kind of thing very funny, Josh. How would you like it if that happened to you?" Tom asked him.

"Are you threatening me?" Josh asked, stepping closer to Tom like a big shot. Tom smiled a dangerous smile.

"I just want you to think about what it's like. I think you owe Adam an apology."

"An apology? Ha! This loser?" Josh stopped talking. He didn't have a clue who he was talking to. His eyes glossed over for a moment.

"What are you doing to him, Tom?" Adam said, looking back to see if Josh's mother was watching.

"Don't worry, he's fine," said Tom. "Now Josh, why don't you apologize to Adam?"

"I'm sorry," Josh said, dead serious, "I'm so sorry."

"And do you think this will happen again?"

"No, of course not. I am so sorry for what we've done to you, Adam," said Josh.

"See how easy that was? That's all we wanted. It wasn't so hard, was it?" asked Tom.

"Can we go now?" asked Adam.

"Of course we can. One more thing Josh, I'm sure you will share with your friends your newfound perspective on life. Isn't that right? You will lead by example?"

"Yes," said Josh.

"And you'll start being nicer to your mother."

"Yes."

"That's it! See how things can be handled without violence?" Tom said to them in the form of a question. He patted them both on the back joyfully, like they were all good friends.

"Let's go," Adam insisted, trying to lead him to the door. They both walked out through the front door of Josh's house and found themselves at Adam's.

"Thank you," said Adam.

"You know I will always be there for you," Tom said.

"No, not for defending me, thank you for not hurting him."

"What? Is that how you see me? I'm sorry. You know I don't want people picking on you," Tom said.

"I am just glad you found a way to do it non-violently. It's nice that we can solve our problems in more productive ways."

"I guess you're right. I don't think it makes much of a difference really, but it seems like we won't get in any trouble for it," Tom said.

A few days later Tom was back in Doctor Fletcher's office waiting for his appointment. When Tom was called for his appointment, he was excited to talk about what had happened. He had followed the Doctor's advice and it went spectacularly. Tom was especially pleased that Adam was happy with him about it. Tom had no qualms with hurting the other students, but Adam was more compassionate at this point in their friendship. A different person walked into the office. It was another dark haired man in a smoking jacket, but it wasn't Doctor Fletcher.

"Good afternoon Tom, I'm Doctor Johnson, I have been working with Doctor Fletcher for many years and I am afraid I have bad news. Doctor Fletcher won't be making it to the appointment today."

"What happened?" Tom asked, with a sense of dread.

"Doctor Fletcher was killed yesterday on his way to the bank. Someone found out he had the winning lottery ticket and killed him for it."

"What?" Tom asked in surprise, shaking his head 'no' impulsively.

"I'm sorry Tom. These things happen in the adult world. I want you to know that I will be taking over his casework and would like you to keep seeing me to talk about this."

"I... I... no. This can't be true. He was fine. He was here."

"I'm sorry Tom. I am here to talk when you are ready. I know you may need some time to process this. We can skip today's session if you think it would be better for you."

"That might be a good idea," Tom said. He needed some time to think about this.

Tom found himself walking back home. He didn't live that far away, but it would give him time to think. Was this his fault? The numbers that Doctor Fletcher wanted... they were for the lottery, weren't they? Tom had to fix this. It was his fault. Could he bring someone back from the dead? No. That seemed like it was too far. He could prevent it though. Time was a man-made concept. That meant he could break it, or at least bend it. Tom closed his eyes and thought of that moment when he wrote the numbers. He pictured it as if he were still there writing.

"Don't think too hard about it," said Doctor Fletcher. Tom had the paper in front of him, writing the numbers. Instead of writing the numbers he had written last time, he changed them. He wrote down the wrong numbers.

Tom opened his eyes. He was still walking back home, but he turned around instead and went back to Doctor Fletcher's office.

"Oh, did you forget something?" the receptionist asked.

"No, is Doctor Fletcher in?" Tom asked her.

"I'm sorry, hold on one second." The receptionist picked up the phone and paged someone. "Can you come to the office? Your three o'clock is back."

"It will just be a moment," she said to Tom. Tom was pacing back and forth in the room as he waited. Doctor Johnson walked into the office again. It still wasn't Doctor Fletcher.

"Tom?" asked Doctor Johnson, "Is there something I can help you with? Do you feel like talking?"

"Where is Doctor Fletcher?" asked Tom.

"I'm sorry, Tom, I know it must be hard. As I already explained to you, Doctor Fletcher was in a car accident on his way home yesterday." It hadn't worked. Doctor Fletcher died anyway. Tom's action had nothing to do with it. It wasn't his fault. He was just a conduit in the other reality. There were things that were meant to happen that Tom would have no control over.

Chapter 12
Source

Tom woke up in his bed the next morning. He still felt residual effects from the drug he had taken. Why had he withheld this memory from himself? Tom felt like he should eat something but he wasn't very hungry. He still felt very light. It was hard for him to get out of bed. His bed was so comfortable. He moved his legs and arms around and wrapped himself up in the blankets. Why did anyone get out of bed in the morning? It felt so good to lie here, instead of getting up. He slept for another hour.

Tom didn't know what time it was, but where did he have to be? It didn't matter. 'I just might stay in bed all day,' he thought to himself. Tom's mind was half awake. He drifted in and out of dreams, not sure what was real, but enjoying it nonetheless. It was almost more fun when it was the dream. He could control things while he was asleep in the same way he used to when he was awake. Tom felt like his usual self while he was dreaming. There was no loss.

Anything that needed to be done in the real world could be done later. What was the hurry? Tom was running through the forest one minute, then back in his bed the next. He dreamed of beautiful things. He could fly through the air once again, over the city or just around his house. Everything was light and fresh. The possibilities were endless. Experiencing this while he slept reminded him of how much he missed the life he used to have control over. Tom had to get his powers back.

There was a time when the dreams stopped. He came out of the euphoria like a headache going away. Most people don't notice it happening. He could feel different parts of his brain being activated. There was a warmth that left when his mind came back to consciousness. Tom knew that meant he wouldn't be going back to sleep this time. The bed was still comfortable and he still laid there thinking about how comfortable everything was. He thought about his dreams and tried to bring himself back into them, not ready to let go of that feeling.

When Tom finally did get out of bed it was already one-thirty. He still had a slight sensitivity to light. Tom took an even longer shower this time than the last time. It just felt so good to have the water pouring over his body.

Tom put the same clothes on again, making a mental note that he really did need to buy more clothes. He had nothing else planned for the day, but he was hungry at this point. Tom decided it would be a good idea to go grocery shopping, this time to get food instead of to occupy time. He made coffee and took it with him in his travel mug. It was a good day for sunglasses. Tom had a nice pair that he put on and stepped outside with his travel mug. Things felt like they were taking a lot more time than they used to. Up until now Tom would blink his eyes and open them somewhere else. Travel by foot and by car had become obsolete when he had a clear destination in mind. (He would fly his car over the city when he was bored or simply filling time.) The rebalancing of his energy was leaving his mind fresh and empty. He didn't feel so burdened by his mind as usual. It was the first time his mind was close to silent since he got his memories back.

Tom spent the remainder of the day shopping and enjoying life like he imagined a retired teenager would. Tom told me there were two highlights of this day that stood out to him. The first was talking to Sam on the phone and setting up a time they could talk tomorrow. The second was a mom and pop bookstore where he found an old copy of The Way of Zen, by Alan Watts. That night he stayed home reading the book while drinking a nice bottle of wine that he had gotten while shopping for groceries. It was a pleasant feeling to have his refrigerator full of fruit and vegetables. He could eat whenever he wanted. It was a luxury he had before, but now it had meaning, because there was the duality involved that came with the option not to have it. Much like air being more valuable to a drowning person. Some things you just take for granted. Tom was really enjoying the time he spent doing things. Everything had been so easy for him before. It felt like he had a new hobby. Tom was delighted that with this newfound responsibility, came a sense of accomplishment. He found this new sensation to be delightful. It actually mattered now whether or not he did things so simple as eating, sleeping, and showering!

"Brilliant!" he said to himself. It suddenly made more sense to Tom why people are the way they are. He hadn't been considering why people asked for the things they did in their wishes up to this point. If these new responsibilities in his life were so big and new, he imagined what it would be like having to worry about everything else too. It all made sense. The more people involved, the more there is to balance, including the introduction of relationships inside of those groups. Mothers would want their children to do well on tests and everyone would worry about money because it allowed them to do everything from the very basics of life to the more complex things, like vacation planning. They have an entirely different idea of what it means to live.

The next day Tom was nervous, but ready to stand his ground. He needed Sam to understand how he felt about getting back his powers. He didn't want to keep it a secret from her, in the way the vision of himself had mentioned.

Tom was too busy being involved with wanting his powers back to really see how good his life was without them. His freedom from everything took away the good parts, as well as the bad. Enjoying the small things. Tom was willing to risk it all by talking to Sam. Though he understood life better at this point, he still didn't realize that it could hold value to him as well. When Sam got there that night, he had cooked dinner for both of them, which was impressive to her (knowing that he actually had to do something for it to happen), even though it was just spaghetti. Tom thought that was a fitting way to start because that is how their date went when they were younger, but this time he had to cook it. Tom knew it wasn't the best spaghetti in the world, or even close, but the gesture was what mattered and if he was going to live like this, even for a short time, he would have to know how to cook.

"There is something important I need to talk to you about," said Tom while they ate dinner. This was after the basic pleasantries, formalities, and stories about one's day. The look on Sam's face changed. It turns out that Tom was one of those people who is bad at bringing things up. It sounded much worse than it was going to be. Sam was worried it was about their relationship, and in a way it was, but not quite as dramatic as her mind was creating.

"What is it?" she asked him, thinking of all the things it could be. Did he meet someone else? Was it going to be too much for him to be with her? What if he found out about… STOP! Her mind was getting out of control. There was so much more it could have thought in those few seconds, but she caught hold of herself and let him speak.

"These last few days have been really hard for me. I think I know how to make it better, but I need your help and I didn't want to hide it from you," Tom said.

"There is someone else, isn't there?" Sam asked him with dread, remembering what had happened.

"What? No. I want my powers back. I am having a hard time feeling the way I used to about everything. I can't let go of things anymore, they stay with me in my head."

"Oh, I see. That's it? You had me worried. You know I'm here for you, if you ever want to talk."

"It's not that. I have thought about it and how my life could go, and the only thing that is missing is my powers."

"If you really think that you won't be happy without them, then I support you in getting them back. I just don't want to lose you, Tom. The new you and the old you. You have become someone I can finally see myself being with again. I know it seems like a lot of weight to have these memories back, but I like that you remember our history and the things we have been through. For the first time I feel like we really get each other, like we are on the same page with everything. If there is a way to get your powers back, and still keep you who you are now, then I am all for it."

"Really?"

"Of course. I was never against your powers, just your unwillingness to be vulnerable with me."

"That is a relief. I was worried you would be against it. I guess I thought that they might make me into someone else. Part of me wanted to hide it from you, but I can't do that anymore. I don't want to lie. I want us to make all of our decisions together. I want us to be able to trust each other."

"Aww, I'm proud of you. I am glad you made the right choice. I support you if you want to get your powers back, and trust that you will remain the person you are now. Do you have any idea where to start?"

"The only thing I can think of is to find the guru and ask him for help. You are the last person I know who saw him, so I was hoping you would help me."

"You know he moves around a lot. He could be anywhere."

"I know, but it is all I have to go on. It is a place to start, even if chances are slim that he is still there."

"Or that I can even find it again. I wandered for quite a while when I was looking for him. We can do this together if you'll let me come with you. I think this will give us a good chance to spend time with each other, even if we don't find what you are looking for. I support you. I will take some of my vacation time to go on this trip. I should have enough money saved for plane tickets."

"Yes! Thank you so much. Don't worry about money babe, I can pay for them."

"You can? You have money saved from working?"

Tom opened the banking app on his cell phone and showed her the balance.

"What? Is that even a number?" Sam asked in surprise, when she looked at his phone.

"What do you mean?"

"It's just so... much."

"Oh. Yeah, I see that now. Back when I had powers I filled the account so I would never have to worry about bills."

"Tom, neither of us ever have to work again with that kind of money. I mean, if you want to spend that much time with me."

"I do, but I don't know if I 'm ready for it yet. I am not happy enough with myself. There are things I need to work through," Tom said. It wasn't just losing his powers, but the weight of their past relationship that he was going to have to work through. They had both done things wrong, but Tom knew that he would have to take the bulk of the responsibility because he had been the one caught with another woman. He had been the one to run. To hide by erasing his memories. It wasn't just the mistakes, it was his unwillingness to deal with them that had been the biggest strain for Sam. It was finally getting better. He could be the person she wanted him to be. He was finally owning up to his past.

Less than a week later they had made their plans to travel across the world in search of the guru.

Chapter 13
Finding the Guru

Tom felt he had been lucky with this turn of events. He had underestimated how much Sam really did care about him and wanted both of them to be happy. Tom was glad he had stuck with truth instead of trying to hide his intentions of getting back his powers. He felt deep down that he would never be truly happy without his powers. It was an egoic attachment once again. Getting there seemed so much harder this time, he was searching after the guru instead of letting the guru find him like last time. There was a great distance to cross and the only power he had to speed it up was the money for a plane ticket and legs to walk with. As the flight progressed, Tom had tears streaming down his face. Sam noticed and asked him what was wrong.

"Are you all right?" she asked.

"Yes," he replied, "I am not crying for any reason, it is simply that when I get closer to him, the love that permeates his whole being starts to push out all of the feelings I have been holding back. It is not something I can help, but it doesn't hurt, it feels freeing. Like I can let go of all the things that are wrong with me. He doesn't judge, he just loves."

"I think I understand. That is how I felt when I was near him too," Sam said.

"It means we're on the right track."

After the nine hour flight, they finally arrived at the airport in the huge country where Sam had last seen the guru. They had to go on foot into the remote village in the mountains. The journey took several days of camping in between walking. It seemed to be taking much longer than usual. For one thing, Tom was not used to flying, or camping, or having to cross vast distances in this fashion. When they finally got to the town, the usual commotion had been filled with silence. There was nobody on the streets this time. The entire marketplace had been deserted. Off in the distance near the river, they heard screaming and chanting, "RAM NAM, SATYA HAI," but they couldn't see what was going on. Tom wasn't concerned with it. He had come to see the guru, and the best place to find him would be the temple. Sam decided she would see what has going on at whatever ceremony was being performed. Witnessing such cultural events was one of the main reasons she liked to travel. Everything was so different everywhere in the world.

As Tom opened the doors of the temple, he could still hear the chanting in the background. It was the first time he had heard people yelling their mantras in such a fashion. There was a strange, heavy air to it, "RAM NAM SATYA HAI, SATYABOL SATYA HAI." As the giant door closed behind him, Tom was left in the pure silence of this place of worship. Where were all the people who gathered here every day? When Tom thought that there wasn't a single person in the temple, a tall man appeared out of the next room with a broom. He must have been sweeping with it before, but was now holding the broom like a trident, as if it were an instrument of great power.

"What's going on?" Tom asked the devotee.

"It is a funeral ceremony. A great saint has left his body," said the man.

Tom felt his stomach fall to the ground. He thought he might throw up. His head was spinning, he knew what this meant.

"He has left us?" Tom asked with a pitiful voice.

"Don't be silly, where could he go? The body is just a vessel, they are burning it by the river. The real guru will always be here with us, in our hearts, in our minds, in places like this. All around us, he has returned to become part of the whole."

"That is why you are still here?"

"Someone has to look after the temple. A place of worship can never truly be empty."

The great doors to the temple cracked open letting in Sam and the chanting of the mob, "RAM NAM, SATYA HAI." Sam stopped immediately when she saw Tom.

"You know?" she asked him.

"Yes, he told me," Tom said, pointing to the space where the man had been. The devotee with the broom had disappeared.

"There is no one here. Everyone in town is gathered by the river," Sam said. Tom realized who it had been.

"Do you want to go to the funeral pyre?"

"No. It is just a body. I'm going to stay here to be with him." Sam went back to the river to watch the ceremony, while Tom stayed in the temple, sitting solemnly by where the guru used to sit. He tried to hold back his tears but quickly realized there was no fighting it. His teacher had left him, and at a great time of need. He must have known that Tom was coming.

"This is where he would be sitting, if this were any other day," said a voice from behind him. The devotee with the broom was back, and Tom had a feeling that no one else would see him.

"It was good of you to come." Tom replied.

"I am here to pay my respects to a great saint."

"So am I," said Tom, "at least, that is all there is left to do."

"He would want us to let go of our attachment to his physical form and remember the love that he preached. That was his message. All love. The greatest miracle of all. When you were with him, it wasn't just that he loved you, it was that he opened you up to love him and everyone else."

"I came here for selfish reasons, but I am glad he let me come," said Tom.

"There are many who will not make it to the celebration, but they are still in his heart. People forget about him, but he never forgets about them. That is just as important. Knowing he is there with you all the time, not just when you are conscious of it." This was the last thing the man said to Tom before their conversation ended.

Tom was left alone sitting in front of the altar with his eyes closed. The tears had stopped. He felt nothing but silence, a heavy emptiness that carried nothing with it. Peace.

Sam held him in her arms that night while his reborn tears faded into sleep. She had only known the guru for a short amount of time, but understood how much he meant to the world and to Tom, who was the world to her.

The next morning, Tom was up before Sam. He was already dressed when she woke up.

"Good morning," she said to him.

"Good morning," he replied, sitting at the edge of the bed.

"Are you okay?"

"As okay as I ever will be. What do we do now?" Tom asked.

"I don't know. I think we have to accept that there may not be a way to get your powers back. He was the gateway, and now he has gone back to wherever it is great people are when they are not on Earth."

"It's not fair. We missed him by two days. We should have gotten here sooner."

"We didn't know. We got here as fast as we could."

"I just wish there was something I could do to make this all better," Tom said.

"So do I. I hate to see you so upset. The flight back is in a few days. We'll have to see what we do from there. You may find that it's not so bad living like everybody else."

Chapter 14
Awakening

On the other side of the world back where Tom and Sam lived out most of their lives, a man in a hospital bed opened his eyes. The world was initially too bright for him to look at. His eyes hadn't been used for a long time. He pushed the call button next to his bed and summoned a nurse.

"Where am I?" he asked the nurse with a scratchy voice when she came in response to the call.

"Oh my. You're awake. I'll send the doctor to come talk to you," she replied.

So many questions came running through his mind, but most obvious of all to him was the awareness that came along with being conscious for the first time in many years.

"Good morning, I'm Doctor Watkins," said the man in the medical coat as he walked in the room, "I'm sure you have a lot of questions. There will be time for them. Right now, we have a few tests to run, and after a few months of physical therapy you will be back in the world as usual."

"What? The car crash? What happened?" asked the patient.

"That's right. You were in an accident. Do you remember everything? Can you tell me your name?"

"I think so. Yes. My name is Adam."

"That's good. We'll go through all of this in the tests. There are a few different people you will need to talk to. There is something I have to tell you, and it may come as a bit of a shock. You have been in a coma."

"A coma? Like asleep?"

"Yes."

"For how long?"

"A little over ten years."

"Huh. I always thought that only happened in the movies..."

"Is there someone we can contact for you?"

"Yes. Well. I don't know. Did anyone survive the crash?"

"If I recall correctly everyone in the car survived. Your sister and the other passenger were hardly touched by the impact."

"Oh. Please don't tell them. I want it to be a surprise... and I don't want her to see me like this."

"I understand. Now, don't try to do things too quickly. Your body is not used to it. Everything will come in time."

Chapter 15

The Shadow Corporation

A few weeks later everything was back to normal. Just normal. Not Tom's normal, but the world's normal. Sam was working again and Tom was hanging around trying to find something he would really want to do with himself if he never got his powers back. After getting back from lunch, Tom opened the door of his house to find a mysterious figure standing in the entry way. Tom was not frightened by it, he was used to his mind bringing and creating people at the will of his ego or subconscious, but this was not someone he had created. He was glad to see that it was not himself, like last time. It was someone real who had come to him. Tom could only see the bottom half of her face; she was a girl close to his age, slightly taller than Sam, wearing all black.

"Hello, Tom, I'm sorry for the intrusion," she said to him, "please have a seat." She motioned to the living room. If anything, this was the most exciting thing that had happened to Tom since he lost his powers, so he was ready and even anxious to be a part of the adventure. If his mind wasn't so wrapped up with Sam, he might have noticed how cute this girl was. He listened to her and took a seat on the couch.

"Thank you," she said. "Tom, we have been watching you for quite some time now." Tom was finding that he had more followers than he knew about. First, the government agent at the bar, and now this. "I am Sarah, of the Shadow Corporation. It is a pleasure to finally meet you, Tom."

"You as well, I suppose," said Tom extending his arm to shake her hand. She paused for a moment then put her hand out to him. Her hand was warm and soft. She had very pretty nails. Tom was getting distracted. It was easy to do when you find an attractive member of the opposite sex mysteriously in your living room.

"What can I do for you?" Tom said, sitting back on the couch and spreading his arms like he owned the place. Technically, he did, but this was clearly a nonverbal que to show it.

"The Shadow Corporation was formed by a group of bioengineers based on the universal manipulation we have seen by beings like yourself. This phenomenon is based on a principle we refer to as the universal manipulation field, it is a field of energy that surrounds living beings, that allows them to do extraordinary things. We have never seen anyone control it the way you did. Our company has spent the last thirty years experimenting with the bioelectric field of human beings and has found a way to stimulate the universal manipulation response."

"You're wasting your time, I have no powers," Tom replied.

"We know. You aren't able to use your powers, but the field around a person never changes so drastically that it goes away completely. Until death, that is. You have just lost your conscious connection with it. It is the perfect time for you to join us. We didn't think that we would have anything to offer you before, but now that has changed. We want to help you and we feel that it would be a beneficial relationship for both of us."

"Why would you want to help me?" Tom asked.

"There is much we have to gain from each other. You want your powers back and we would like the opportunity to study you and the data around your biorhythmic activity. The potential scientific advances in your case study would be unparalleled."

"Why the cloak and dagger routine?"

"Oh, you mean the outfit? Let's just say that our work isn't exactly approved of by people in high places. They are either afraid of what we can make people into or they want to exploit us to win wars. We are above that kind of thinking. We want our progress to benefit mankind, not detract from it. Only the people we think we can help are aware of our existence. There are a few groups like ours, none of them as advanced or as cohesive. We have buildings on top of buildings on top of buildings, that act as our cover. This is very high level security clearance that we are offering you, to even be told about our existence, yet alone the kind of details we are willing to share with you."

"I'm flattered, I think. So you will help me to get my powers back? How do we begin?" Tom asked.

"Unfortunately it isn't as easy as a nine to five job. You will have to come with us for... as long as it takes. We are very private in what we do, and for good reason. If everything goes according to our estimates, it will only take a few months before you are back into your regular routine, whatever you may want that to be. We have a core group of scientists that have been dedicated to your case. Needless to say, you have been an anomaly in what you have accomplished. We are very eager to see what you will be able to do with our assistance, and the data it will provide could be beneficial for generations to come," Sarah said.

"I will need time to think about it and discuss this with my girlfriend."

"Ah, yes. Sam. Don't worry, you will have time. We know you may need to get your affairs in order before joining the company. Please bear in mind that we do wish to retain anonymity. Beyond even the government, there are other radical groups that are after our research. If anyone else contacts you about your powers let us know immediately. It could be dangerous. As for Sam, it is partially for her protection that she can't know about our existence. You won't be able to tell her where you are going or with whom. If we suspect that you are sharing secrets you will never hear from us again. I know that is the one thing that will get through to you. Getting your powers back is within your grasp, don't waste this opportunity."

"I understand. How can I contact you?" Tom asked.

"There is no need. We already have Seer-ers, people with sight beyond sight. It it so much more cohesive than using outdated technology like gps and hidden cameras. We already know the exact moment you will be ready and I am already there to pick you up. This conversation never would have taken place if we thought there was a chance you would say no."

"Hmph. I think I've made people feel this way before. I never knew what it was like. It is not so pleasant being on this side of the conversation. I'll see you soon then, from how you make it sound," said Tom.

"Yes. It was nice to meet you, Tom. A lot of us in the company look up to you, and have followed your work. We had to draw straws for which one of us would get to talk to you. I won. Don't take this the wrong way, but I have been dreaming about meeting you my whole life. You mean so much to the company. You are a legend back at the Shadow Corporation."

"How should I take it?" Tom asked.

"Heh. I guess it doesn't leave a lot of room for interpretation." Sarah put her hand to her temple for a moment then quickly became more serious. "I have to go now. Until we meet again." She gave him an excited hug and then was gone before Tom could blink. This could be the answer. A way to get his powers back. The universe provides.

Chapter 16
The Talk & The Cowboy

Tom prepared for his next big talk with Sam. He would need to ask for time away from her, even though the motivation was not to be away from her, but to get back his powers. It would be difficult not telling her everything, but Sarah had made it clear he had to keep it a secret. It was a lot of trust to ask for, so soon in their new relationship. Sam agreed to stop by after work that day to talk to him. When she got to his house their conversation went something like this:

"Hi sweetie, how was your day?" Sam said to him.

"Not too bad, I've been doing a lot of thinking. How about you?" Tom asked.

"Pretty good. It was nice to be back in the field, there is a lot of work to be done, people to protect. I forgot how much I enjoy it. What is it you wanted to talk about?"

"Well, as you know, I have been feeling lost lately. I thought I would be able to get help from the guru, but when I found out he was gone I thought all hope was lost. I think I may have another way."

"If it's going to help, you know I support you."

"I know. The thing is, it is something I have to do on my own. I need to go on this search to find myself and what I have lost."

"How long will it take?"

"I don't know. Hopefully not too long. I know we have just started to rebuild our relationship and I hope this doesn't have a negative impact. I want you to know that I am coming back and that you will be in my heart the whole time."

"Tom, I don't know if I can... I mean, if I don't even know how long you'll be gone. We just started getting things back together. How can you expect me to wait for you?"

"I guess I can't, but I really hope you do. I am asking you to trust me, and I know it is a lot to ask."

"I want to, I really do, but I can't do it if you won't even tell me how long you'll be gone. It wouldn't be fair to me. It is still hard to trust you after all that has happened between us. What if one of us meets someone and the other is left hanging?"

"That won't happen."

"Can't you keep in touch somehow?"

"I don't think so. I have to be completely cut off from everything. I will need space and time to make progress. I only pray that it is enough to get my powers back."

"I hope so too, babe. I know you need this and I won't stop you. I'll try to be here when you get back."

"Thank you for understanding. I know it's not easy, but you have to believe me. I really do love you, and I think we have a future together. Even when I didn't have my memories I still felt a connection with you. This is real."

"I want that to be true, I really do, and I hope you find what you need," said Sam.

She seemed to be taking it harder than he had hoped. Tom didn't blame her for it, but couldn't help but feel bad that he did not feel the same way. He imagined this is what she was talking about when she said he didn't quite understand her feelings. Tom didn't feel like he was giving her up by leaving because of his closeness to her. He knew exactly where he would be going and what that meant. He wished he could share it with her. In his mind, there was never any doubt about his feelings for her, and it hurt that it was even an issue. He had gone through his mind and found that she was on top of the list. Nothing would ever come between them again, once he got his powers back.

He didn't want this to come off the way it did. It was asking a lot for this kind of trust. Sam was right in thinking that he was putting his powers before her, but she also felt that this meant he didn't care enough about her to be completely open. There was a strange idea that if you weren't the only thing someone cared about, then they didn't care at all. This wasn't the case. It was always easier to compare instead of being happy with the love that was given. There could always be more from this person or from someone else.

The mind keeps on comparing. It always creates what is not there instead of accepting what is and enjoying it. Once you have the same meal every day you start to take it for granted, it loses the newness, the enjoyment it had the first time you tried it. This is the mind. It wants more and more and makes sure that you keep on wanting so that you can be attached. To a clear mind, the love that Sam and Tom had for each other was beautiful and enough for both of them. When you are inside of the situation and the mind takes over, nothing is ever enough. The mind keeps wanting more and telling you that it is possible. It brings in the future and the past, then creates a comparison. It creates meaning for the things that are happening, instead of letting them happen as they are and enjoying it. There is much more to say, but time is running short, and I must get back to Tom's story before he tells me again to get on with it.

The next day Tom woke up on time. He was ready and excited, as long as he didn't think about how this might make Sam feel. He enjoyed his bed for a little while, then his shower and coffee. When he stepped outside, a limousine was waiting for him. Sarah was leaning against it. She was still wearing all black, as per usual. She had a dark ponytail and a cute face. Most people Tom's age would be hard pressed not to be attracted to her.

"I'm glad you made it," Sarah said.

"You say that like I had a choice," Tom replied, smiling and going in for a hug. That seemed to be the proper greeting now, since their last conversation had ended that way.

"Sometimes it's fun to act like things are unexpected. It makes me feel normal," Sarah said.

"I know what you mean. It can be more pleasant to play the game than to be involved with what you know is going to happen."

"Yes, exactly, but I'm sure you'll be happy to be in a position where you are the one choosing for that to happen."

"You've got that right," Tom said.

"Get in, they're waiting for us at the lab," Sarah said, opening the car door for him.

Tom got in the back of the limo with Sarah and they drove off down the street.

"Aww, no champagne?" Tom asked as Sarah got in.

"It's not that kind of limo," Sarah replied with a grin, "and alcohol mutes the biofield."

Ten miles away, Sam was walking to lunch. She was outside a sandwich shop, when she noticed an old man walking into the street. There was a bus coming and he was sure to be run over. Sam threw her hands up and back over her head. The old man was pulled to the sidewalk just in time for the bus to speed by where he had been standing. Sam ran over to the old man to see why he hadn't been paying attention, but when the man got up, he wasn't an old man anymore. He had changed into a tall, dark-haired man, who was now dressed as a cowboy. He had snake-skin boots and a ten gallon hat, a denim button down shirt with a bolo and blue jeans. He looked as though he hadn't shaven in a few days, very rugged. Sam was surprised that the appearance of the man had changed in such a dramatic fashion. There was no possibility of recognizing him as the same person, if she hadn't been staring directly at him.

"Thanks, little girl, I knew you had it in you," he said.

"What? Had what in me? Who are you?" Sam asked.

"Name's Jack. I know how you saved me just now. You have the power."

"What power?"

"I don't think there's a name for it. Just some kind of energy surrounding certain ones of us that allows us to do incredible things. I have it too. When I was young a man named Howard taught me how to connect with these natural powers of existence."

"So what is it you want?" Sam asked.

"I want to help you to learn to use these powers. It is a terrible thing to waste."

"But I don't... I don't have any powers..."

"Oh, yes you do. I knew it from the moment I saw you. That's why I stepped in front of that bus. I had a feeling you would save me. Traumatic events, and moments of great emotional intensity allow this energy to come out more freely. Scientists attribute it to adrenaline, but that's just a way of oversimplifying what they don't understand. It's a strange thing really. Having a clear mind is what really allows it to happen, and those moments of extreme stress make it hard for the mind to act and interpret, so there is silence."

"How did you find me?" Sam asked.

"Intuition."

"Alright," Sam said. At this point in her life, she was used to these kinds of things happening. Who knows what could happen, not to mention the cowboy was attractive, even though he was noticeably older than she was. She did have time to explore new things, now that Tom wasn't around, and if she could have powers like him... maybe they would have more in common. "When do we begin?" She asked.

"As soon as you are ready."

"It just so happens that my schedule is free, except for work. Let's start tomorrow evening."

"Works for me. Come to this address when you are ready." He handed her a business card with an address on it. She smiled at him and they parted ways.

Chapter 17
Entering the Shadows

Tom wasn't exactly sure where the building they took him to was located. It must have been somewhere downtown, judging by the size. There was floor after floor of research facilities, and a wing with living quarters. They showed Tom the room he would be occupying when he wasn't busy with their research. It was a small room with minimal luxuries. They told him the less that he had, the better, because there was less chance of attachment. The energy field was dampened by attachment to worldly possessions and ideas. They distracted the mind and took away from the silence. There was a beautiful garden for meditation. Sarah showed Tom around the whole building and introduced him to the members of the team he would be working with.

"Before we begin anything complex," said Sarah, "take this." She handed him a small red pill.

"What is it?" said Tom, taking it from her.

"It's a mood stabilizer. We have noticed that the biorhythmic field is sometimes blocked or uncontrollable with extreme emotion on either end of the spectrum. So we try to keep ourselves in the middle where everything is perfect. The more in control you are of your emotions and attachments, the less you will need any assistance from such things as the mood stabilizers. Now let's get a full scan of you and your biorhythmic field so we can determine what is blocking your universal manipulation energies."

Tom followed her into a laboratory. There was a table for him to lie on while being scanned. He saw the scientist he had met earlier behind the control panel. Tom didn't remember the man's name but it was something with a T. He didn't feel any different than normal. Tom was not prone to extreme emotions most of the time. There was an occasional swing up or down when he was off of his powers, but that felt like an exception to the rule. He didn't know it, but most of the cloudiness of his mind came from his relationship with Sam. An attachment that he may never be ready to let go of. The machinery began humming and light passed over his body. The whole process took about ten minutes, then they showed him the results on their computer.

"Everything looks great," said the scientist.

"Wow," said Sarah, "your energy is extraordinary. It looks like it has been growing." They had taken a scan of him before, but he didn't know it. It had been over a distance with the help of the seers.

Tom didn't know what he was looking at. It was an outline of a human surrounded by a green and blue light.

"According to this reading, there are only small blockages," said Sarah, "most of it must be mental."

"I don't know if that is a surprise or not," Tom said.

"The good news is we can clear these right up and get you practicing. The mood stabilizers should help a little, but most of it will be through your own peace of mind."

"The age old question," Tom said, "how to find peace of mind."

"There have been many advancements in that field. They have been studying things like meditation for centuries. Have you ever meditated? We have been perfecting their methods here, as well as researching the more raw aspects of it."

"So where do we start?" Tom asked.

"We will have to silence your mind. Well, you have to learn to do that I mean. We have ways of doing it but they are usually rejected by the host... in not so nice ways. The best way is going to be to work through the things that are bothering you. Anything that you are holding on to that you feel is right or wrong you will have to let go. Those ideas are attachments. If you have anything you love or hate, you will have to let go of those ideas as well. Any extreme emotion must be worked through and understood, or it will dominate your thinking."

Tom knew that meant most of the memories he had gotten back. They all had something attached to them. Maybe he should ask them if they could erase them for him. No. That would be the easy way out. He would lose Sam. That was his ego talking.

"We have plenty of space for you to relax and spend time with your mind," said Sarah, "everything you need is at your disposal. Any time you are ready to try to use your manipulation field, let me know. I will show you some of the small puzzles that we have developed and then we can work our way up to the more advanced techniques."

"Thank you," said Tom, "you guys have been very kind to take me in like this. It was more than I could have asked for."

"It's quite the opposite, Tom. We are blessed to have you here with us. You are an inspiration to us all. Half of what we know is possible, is because we saw you do it. We want as much as you do to get your powers back," Sarah said.

"It's nice to feel like I have a place where I am accepted for who I am. Somewhere I can be myself without others being afraid of me."

"You can call me any time you need me. There is a communication's system that allows us to reach anyone in the building," Sarah said.

Tom was left to roam around the sections of the building that didn't require higher clearance. If he had his powers he would know everything that was going on there, but for him, there was still much to discover. Everyone had been very friendly. There were other students that he would catch acting like they weren't watching him when he saw them. Sarah made it sound like he was some kind of hero to them. It had just been life as usual to him. He knew it was unusual to be able to do the things he did, but he always accepted it as reality, never anything special.

They made it sound like it would be easier than he imagined to get his powers back. He might get back to Sam sooner than expected. Sam. He loved her. It was an attachment. Tom knew that he would need to learn to love without attachment. Without expectation. Love was greater than that. If he could experience his love unconditionally, then he would be able to do it without attachment and use his powers at will. The other memories had something to do with it too though. Every small moment when something felt right or wrong, he was holding on. Some would be easier to let go than others. There had been things to consider, like bullies in school, but above that was the car crash, and his fight with Adam. He had to make amends with his mother for his father's death and having gone so long without speaking to her.

Tom spent the next few weeks opening his connection with the universal manipulation field. His access was getting greater and greater after the hours he spent working his way through his memories and understanding them. He was starting to know what people were going to say before they spoke.

Little things were starting to seep into his consciousness the more and more he let go of his associations. He swore that he was floating a little the last time he was walking through the garden. They had someone giving him a massage every morning. A masseuse who specialized in the small physical blockages he needed to work through. It was like a day spa for universal manipulators. They were encouraged to interact, but to limit what they said to small talk, if they did talk at all. If they said too much, it could lead to more associations and attachments, thus setting them back, but being around others like him was beneficial.

Tom was having the time of his life in between working his way through the memories. Some of the harder ones he would talk to Sarah about. It was a blessing to have her there with him. He felt like he could open up to her without worrying about judgement. She accepted his feelings gracefully and gave him alternatives to the meaning that the mind had created. Even pointing out that a lot of it was created by his mind was a big step toward understanding. Some of the things Tom was attached to were ideas that what happened meant something. The meaning was his meaning, not the universe. It was an interpretation of the mind. Once he understood that there was no inherent meaning in things and occurrences, he would be able to let go of them.

Chapter 18
Lesson Number One

Miles away in the city, Sam had a response from the tech department at the bureau. She had given them a photo of Jack that she had obtained from the security camera of one of the nearby buildings where they had met. She wanted to know who he was, and why he had suddenly appeared in her life. The tech department had bad news for her. Well, not that bad, more like no news. Jack couldn't be found in the database. He had no identification. He didn't exist. He was a ghost. His identification had been wiped clean, but that could mean any number of things. She was no better off now than she was yesterday, as far as knowing anything more about him.

After work, Sam went to the address that Jack had given her and knocked on the door. It was a steel door that looked like it didn't lead anywhere. There was no signage or windows on the building. Part of her thought it would be best to leave now or call for backup, but she was intrigued by the mystery, and thought that Jack had good character from their first meeting. Except for stepping in front of a bus. Sam was ready for her first lesson, but she wanted some answers first. She wanted to make sure this person was legitimate as a teacher, and that she wasn't wasting her time with a con artist. Just that he knew about it should have been enough of an indication for her, but she was trained to be suspicious. The door opened and Jack was standing there in his cowboy outfit.

"Ahhh, Agent [REDACTED], how nice of you to show up. I'm glad you could make it. Come on in."

"I need to ask you some questions first," Sam said.

"All in due time, we can talk inside. You never know who could be listening out here."

"I need you to talk to me first..." Sam was interrupted by her phone. It was her superior officer, the man Tom had met in the bar. She excused herself from Jack and answered the phone.

"Agent [REDACTED] do you know who this is?"

"Yes sir. Why are you calling me? The higher ups never deal with agents directly."

"We know what you're doing. Jack is an old buddy of ours. We used to call him The Cowboy. He has the highest level clearance. Don't try to find out any more of his past. It is classified. Just know that you can trust him."

The line clicked as the other agent hung up the phone. Sam put down her phone and looked at Jack. He was still grinning at her like he always did, like he was in on a joke.

"Alright," she said, walking through the doorway, "but I want answers eventually."

"Like I said, in due time," Jack replied to her, "for now let's stick to the fun stuff. Like your training."

Walking in the building was rather unremarkable. It was a long hallway with no windows that led to a door at the end. Jack took her through the final door which led to a large room of serenity.

"This is the room of serenity," Jack said. It was a peaceful room that felt like Florida. There were cables that sprayed mist every so often and new age music playing on the speakers around the room. The room was decorated with large fluffy pillows, and cushions to sit on, all of them in a circle.

"This is where our training will be held," Jack said, "it is meant to keep your mind and body in a place of peace.

Choose the pillow you like and have a seat. Then we will begin." Sam picked a cushion and sat down. Jack sat across from her and sat silently for a few minutes before beginning his speech.

"Our philosophy is that the energy power we have is activated by states of extreme emotion. We will guide you to these places so that you will be able to understand them. Once you know what they are like, you will be able to bring them to the surface at will, and manipulate the world in ways that are reflected by that feeling. Our theory is that mind follows body. When the mind goes through an emotion the body follows, and vice versa. The mind reinforces that which it believes is happening. So if you are upset you will be more willing to do things that an upset person would do, instead of things a happy person would do. Part of it is selective attention, it is easier to see bad things when you are unhappy, but we believe it is not that simple. It is not just that you see those things, but that the mind creates them through the energy you dispel. So if you are unhappy, your energy field will actively create more things that will encourage this feeling, thus keeping you in that state and dragging you further into it. That is how we will help you direct your power, by selecting different emotions to activate it. Different things can happen based on the emotion you experience. If you are in states of extreme happiness, it will cascade onto those around you, making it easier to relate to others and get what you want from them. If you are scared, then you will be more in tune with your teleportation abilities. If you are angry, you will be more likely to push energy away from you, throwing objects across the room with your mind. Every emotion does something different, and manifests itself differently in different people. In fact, it can manifest in different ways for you because emotions are a lot more complex than just one direction. Different blends of emotions will create different things. Is all of this making sense?" Jack asked.

"Yes. It does in theory. I don't know about in action, but go on," Sam replied.

"That is normal. You haven't had a chance to see a lot of this, though you did save me from the bus and you were around Tom for a good part of your life."

He knew about Tom? How could she trust him?

Jack continued, "Our first practice is going to be bringing yourself to different emotions through your memories and created memories.

When you start to feel the energy coming on, notice how it appears in your body. Notice where and how each emotion feels to your body, because you will be able to focus on that and bring it back up when you are having a hard time getting the feelings into your mental state. It will eventually become second nature to you. These different states of extreme emotion help to open up the connection to your energy by blocking the mind. The mind is somehow oblivious to the fact that it will lose control if you go deeply into your emotion. It will not know how to react, leaving you with a moment of clarity. Take advantage of that moment and witness what it feels like. Over time you will be able to achieve that clarity all the time, leaving the mind as a servant and doorway to using the energy all around you. It is good to do different mind clearing exercises, such as meditation. There are many different methods that can be used to get you to the same place."

Sam sat there with her mind wandering. What he was talking about was very foreign to her. The bureau had taught her alertness, but it was through constant analysis of the situation and environment. Anything that could happen had to be considered before and during raids and field missions. Her mind could go a million miles a minute, all around every part of the scene. If this guy thought it was as easy as being emotional to keep her mind silent then BANG! Jack clapped his hands together in front of her face. Her body had frozen.

"See? It is easy to stop the mind. Anything that comes up unexpectedly will do the trick. Mind doesn't know how to react, but it does start to build a tolerance. The more I clap in front of you, the more you will start to think about it happening, that it has happened, what it is like. Mind will bring up the past and the future and get more involved in it with every event."

It worked. There was a moment of clarity. It was possible. Could she do this? Would it be that easy?

"Easy might be the wrong word for it," Jack said, seeing what she was thinking, "it could take anywhere from a moment, to many lifetimes. You are already ahead of most people, with the powers you have displayed. So let's start simple. Close your eyes and relax. Try to keep your thoughts at a minimum. Now visualize the first big memory that comes up to you. Do not react to it, just go as deep as you can into it. Then notice where you are feeling the memory."

Sam closed her eyes and relaxed. Thoughts went through her mind. She saw the bagel that she had for breakfast. It had been tasty. What would she do tomorrow? How long would this take. She saw these questions arise and let them pass without interacting. The room was very comfortable. Hopefully it would be a good memory that arose. It went on like this for what seemed like a long time, but had only been a few minutes, before some of her deeper memories started to open up. She found herself in the bedroom of their old apartment. The apartment she had been living in with Tom, after the accident. Her heart was pounding as she reached for the doorknob of the door to their bedroom. She already knew what was there because it was all part of her memory.

"There, I think you've found something," Jack said from far away, "focus on what your body is feeling."

It was like she was there all over again, at the scene of the crime. Her head was spinning.

"Try to keep control over yourself, concentrate on what your body is feeling, not the meaning."

Her legs felt weak, she was in a state of panic over what she was going to find there. There was a heavy weight in her stomach that felt like it would pull her down to the floor or hurl itself forward like a rocket. She could feel her own heart beating rapidly, forcing blood throughout her whole body. Her head was pulsing to the beat. There was a tingling in the back of her head that seemed to be related to the tears she was ready to spew. Her throat felt tight, like she wouldn't be able to take in the next breath, her vocal chords were tense, ready to let out a yell of anguish. She was doing her best to focus on her body and where the feelings were when the door was pulled out of her hands by Tom opening it from the other side, with his shirt still on the floor. There was a girl's voice in the background. She lost her focus, getting too involved in the memory. She came back to the peaceful room with a yell and sent Jack flying across the room.

"I'm sorry," Sam said to him, choking back her emotions.

"Don't be, that was awesome! See the power that you have in you? We're off to a great start, notice where you got lost. What did it feel like?"

"I was watching the different sensations throughout my body, when my focus started fading. It felt like a wave of energy over my whole body, like I was watching it from a foot away from myself. I wasn't there anymore, there was no control."

"Yes. This is great. You're doing great. I think we've gone into it enough for one day, spend the next twenty-four hours remembering what it felt like in your body. Practice it at home, but make sure there is nothing around that you don't mind breaking. We'll start with another memory tomorrow and try to bring up some of the more pleasant energies."

"Can I do it again now?" Sam asked.

"Yeah, if you're up for it. Do you want to do the same thing or something new?"

"Let's see where the mind takes us," Sam said, having gotten her first real taste of this energy. She closed her eyes again and went through the same boring thought processes, thinking about what to have for dinner that night, maybe she should ask Jack out. No, she loved Tom. Stop arguing, let go, let it come naturally, don't get involved. Is that me thinking? Whose voice is in my head? I don't feel like it's me.

The next memory started to arise in her being. It took her out of the room and back to her first date with Tom. She knocked on the door once again, this time it was the door of his childhood home, where there was spaghetti in the basement waiting for her. She skipped ahead to the moment they were watching a movie and getting ready to have their first kiss.

"Good," said Jack's voice once again. "Feel what is occurring in your body."

She felt heat in her chest, where her heart was. Her head was light and empty. She still felt the light tingling in the back of her head, like she might shed a single tear of joy. The base of her tailbone felt like someone was pressing against it. Pressure in her lower spine. In her memory she closed her eyes and felt his lips press against hers for the first time.

Jack clapped his hands, shocking her out of it. She fell to the ground, Sam didn't know it, but she had been floating. She shook herself off with a grin still on her face and a dreamy look in her eyes.

"How was it?"

"It was strong... but I was in control."

"That is how it is with the more enjoyable emotions. It is harder to get lost in them. That is why love is so much more valuable. It is harder to go so deep into it, but when you do there is so much more power. You'll have to practice bringing back these feelings by focusing on your body and where the sensations occur. Then you can have them in this reality instead of in your memories. That way you will be aware of your surroundings, including floating above the ground and the other people around you that will be affected by your energy. This is going splendidly."

"I feel the same way. Can we do it one more time?" Sam asked.

"I like your persistence. That kind of dedication is what you need to really build up your abilities."

Sam closed her eyes and observed. Her body was filled with warmth and light as she thought about the guru and the time she had spent there with him. She could hear the chanting that was going on at the temple twenty-four hours a day. Sam got lost in the love.

"I can really feel that," Jack said, "what are you thinking about?"

"Bhagwan. The guru. The ultimate supreme being. A saint in his own right. There are beings like this that you can sense are not from this world. They are just visiting and every moment with them is one of love," Sam replied.

"It is beautiful," said Jack.

"It gives hope, this knowledge that there is something greater out there that can make us feel this way."

Sam sat in front of the guru in the temple, watching him throwing fruit around to the other devotees. Everyone was trying to sit closer to him. Some were rubbing his feet. He was smiling and laughing, wrapped up in his blanket. Inside was the entire universe. Sam bowed before him and swayed with the music when she was sitting up. It was enchanting. The most beautiful, divine experience she had ever come across. The scene changed into the funeral pyre, where she stood watching them burning the body. She felt his hand slip into hers while she was watching the fire. He was there with her even though his body was no longer occupied. He was set free. She was tearing up once again with the overwhelming love and bliss that everyone felt when they were in his presence. When she opened her eyes, she saw Jack staring at the ceiling wide-eyed with his mouth hanging open. He was experiencing the same thing she was. That was the power of love, of this great being who was always with her. Jack was making loving noises at the overwhelming sensations he was feeling. He started reaching his hands out grasping for the visions that were fading. His breath became heavy. He took in air as deeply as he could.

"Wow," Jack said, "that was incredible."

"I know, but it takes a lot out of you. In a good way. I feel completely drained. What a rush. An emotional rollercoaster. I haven't taken the time to think about these memories. The last one is so recent, but it feels like home. As if it happened outside of time," Sam said.

"Do you want to keep going?" Jack asked her again, looking more expectantly this time. The memory he had just been a part of was like a drug. It was impossible to get enough of it. That unconditional love.

"All right, one more." Sam replied.

She closed her eyes, with warmth and light still in her body. Where did Tom go? Did she trust him? When would he be back? The mind was poking at her, knowing which buttons to press to get her attention. It wasn't very happy that she was gaining control. Is he thinking about you? What if he is with some other woman. He would never do that. But he had done that.

"Ugh," Sam said to herself.

"Let it pass," Jack said, "the mind knows how to get your attention away from the present moment, you have to stay impartial to what it is saying. Don't get involved, become an observer."

Sam kept sitting there, letting her mind say what it wanted to, but this time she didn't get involved with it. She did not let any feelings arise based on what it said to her. She opened her eyes and found herself in a car hurdling down the road, well above the speed limit. Her heartbeat sped up, that was the first thing she noticed. Her eyes were big, everything was bright even though it was night. Tom and Adam were in the front seat arguing.

"We used to do things together, then you threw me out for my sister," Adam said.

"It's not like that," Tom replied, "I still care about you too."

"Then why don't we ever do things together? It looks like I'm finally getting your attention."

"Slow down, you are out of control."

"I'm out of control? You're out of control! The things you did to those kids, you dare tell me that I don't have any control?"

"I was protecting you!" Tom shouted.

Sam noticed her breathing was shallow. She was getting more and more involved in the memory. Things slowed down, every second felt like an eternity. The headlights from the other car were piercing through the windshield into their eyes. Tom was the first to see it, while Adam was staring at him arguing, he didn't know what was about to happen. Sam was helpless, there was nothing she could do to stop it. For a brief moment Tom held up his hands to Adam and this time Sam could see some kind of energy transferring to him right before the weightless sensation of the car flying as it was struck head-on. Sam was jerked back into the real world with a blast of fiery light all around her. Jack shielded himself from it with his hands and an invisible barrier.

"I'm sorry," Sam said to him quickly. The pillows were singed and still smoking.

"Stop apologizing," Jack said, "this is what we are here for. This is a safe place to do these things. Remember, you can't blame anyone else for these feelings, they are all created inside of you, by you. Some situations will inspire certain feelings to arise, but it is up to you whether or not you take their lead. That way you can stay in control through the good and bad, and bring up your energy responsibly."

"Tell me, I saw Tom transferring energy to Adam the second before the car crash we were in as kids, and he is in a coma. Could that have anything to do with it?"

"Transferring energy? I don't know. We don't have a lot of experience with that yet. It could mean any number of things. It is possible that he was trying to protect him, but yes, it is also possible that Adam is in a coma because of him." Jack had seen the vision and the details of Sam's life had come into his mind so that he could better understand where she was coming from.

"Why would he do that? Let Adam suffer, I mean. Why didn't he save him?" Sam asked.

"Those are questions you will have to ask him. I think we've done enough for one day. Meet me here the same time tomorrow, we'll keep going further. You are doing a very good job so far. Some people never manifest their energy in such a direct fashion. I bet your biorhythms are off the chart."

Chapter 19
Falling Down

Then Tom crashed. "It happens to the best of us," is what they told him afterward. His mind had fought back too hard. Every time Tom's mind used it's hidden power to distract him, it would get weaker. The reason is that Tom knew what to expect from it. He became conditioned to expect the response and was ready to deal with it. The more the mind fought against him, the stronger he could fight it, and vice versa. It was all about allowing things to happen. Tom let these feelings come, even though he didn't know why they were coming. It was one last hurrah, a struggle of his mind to take control. It was an ultimatum to his real being by his imagined self. He locked himself in his room and played ZHU's Faded, Odesza remix on repeat for two hours. He sat in weird places and positions with his mind spinning wildly. "Why don't I sit on the floor more often," he asked himself, "it is such an interesting viewpoint." He would laugh while he was crying for no reason, and scream as loud as he could. Sarah came pounding on his door as these thoughts were flashing through his head. She tried to yell over the music: "Tom! Are you all right! What's going on?"

"Nothing!" Tom screamed back, "I'm fine! I'm working through it! Go away!"

Tom's whole body was shaking. He had a hard time seeing through his tears. He smashed his fist into the wall and laughed maniacally while the tears were still coming. His breathing was hard, fast, and shallow.

Sarah had already gotten security at this point. They could get through the door and restrain him. They smashed into the room when their electronic override keys failed. Tom's mind had fried the circuits in the locks.

They found Tom staring up at them from the corner screaming. The furniture was three feet off the ground. The window smashed and the guards were hurled out of the room as the music got louder and louder.

"Get out!" Tom screamed.

"We need a backup, and a medic," the guards reported through the comms system, hoping they could be heard over the music. Everything came crashing down to the floor and Tom threw himself through the now open window. Expecting to fall and land hard on the pavement below, Tom closed his eyes and braced himself, but the fall was short. On the other side of the window was an observation room. They had been watching him from the start. Tom grinned and began laughing uncontrollably as he looked at the window and understood. It wasn't real.

A crowd of all the other students had gathered because of the commotion. Guards in riot gear were storming into the hall.

"No!" Sarah put out her hand to stop them, "I will take care of this." She climbed through the window and slowly made her way toward Tom who scooted backward a few times then hit a wall. She held out her hand to him.

"It's okay, Tom, everything is going to be alright."

"Turn off the music!" one of the guards ordered.

"Can you hear me Tom?" she said, putting her hands on his face and looking in his eyes. Tears kept falling down his face as he looked at her and smiled.

"It's Major Tom," he said to her, and kept on laughing as he cried.

"Tom, you have to take this," she said handing him a white pill. The music was cut off. The whole floor was silent beside the sobbing laughs and gasps of Tom from the other side of the window. The guards stood with their weapons raised. Tom took a deep breath and grabbed on to Sarah, hugging her tightly. She could feel him shaking. She hugged him back. They fell through the floor without disturbing a tile, and landed in the observation room below. There was no one in it.

"Are you okay, Tom?" she asked. "The treatment is working. Look at what you just did!"

"I know. I *know*. I know I know I know," Tom said, still sobbing and laughing. He let out a long deep breath. "Haahhhh. That was intense. Ha ha ha ha. It's ego. It has to put up a fight for it's life, you know?" He was looking at her with a smile, his eyes now calm while his body still shook.

"Are you okay now?" she asked.

"I think so. He he he. I'm getting there. It was a lot to deal with." Sarah used the comms to call off the alert. They could both sense that a crowd was gathering outside of this room as well, but it would go away in time.

"Will you stay with me?" Tom asked through his tears, looking at her like a sad puppy.

"If you want me to," she replied, gently rubbing her hand through his hair.

"I do. I know you! I figured it out. I. Know. You," he smiled and pointed at her when he said, "You."

"I thought you might. Does that change anything for you?"

"Only for the better."

Sarah smiled. "Good." She kissed him on the forehead and held him in her arms for the rest of the night. As he lay there, he started to feel safe from himself. The droning sound of an air-powered organ started in his head, the sound of the devotees in the temple paying their respects to the guru. Tom was filled with warmth and light. The negativity seemed to drop out of him.

Tom's power had been greatly increased by the incident. He had skipped four levels of training and had moved on to phase shifting. He had worked through a major blockage that had formed in his mind.

The students didn't look at him the same way anymore. Neither did the security officers. They would talk behind his back about what had happened. Their hero was as vulnerable as anyone else, even if he could control the universe freely. It didn't bother Tom. They could think whatever they wanted. It was how he reacted to it that was important. That is what created mind blocks. Having an attachment to what things mean, instead of accepting what is really there. As far as Tom was concerned, they looked at him. They didn't look at him with this feeling or that meaning, they just looked and then looked away. No meaning. Meaning was created by ego. He was really starting to understand existence. What you think of me is none of my business.

During his next training session, Sarah was there to guide him through his new skills.

"You have to remember, there is no you. There is nobody. The body is just a container for your energy. It has to exist so that you can translate the energy into something recognizable on this plane. Beyond this reality, there are no constraints such as time, space, and the laws of physics. They are all part of what lets you exist here. Not all of them can be broken, but they can all be bent once you understand their fundamental nature. The energy that makes up the real you, the whole universe, everyone, is not limited by these man-made rules. The mind holds on to them so that it can keep control over your energy, it is even why we are here in the first place. With the ability to do everything, there is no challenge; nothing for the energy to do. So when it decides, the energy takes human form and goes through the actions and karmas that it would not be able to go through in the ethereal realm. It is a form of entertainment, a game, a play. They call these events 'leela.' None of it has any meaning, it is just something to do. So let go of this reality, but don't get lost from it. This is where you have to come back, until it is your time to move on. Many people have gone crazy or suffered a terrible fate from losing themselves during this kind of experimentation. That is why many people are afraid of the methods that are used to attain freedom. Freedom is not about losing the self completely, but about understanding it and observing it. You need to realize that there is no self, but one greater whole. Our goal is not to get rid of it, but to coexist. Use of chemicals can bring you to these places, but many people are not ready for that leap, so they have a hard time dealing with the truth."

"I understand," Tom replied, "so where do we start?"

"Today is going to be a fun day! We are going to work on temporal movement. The training you have received up until now has prepared you for this step, which you did so freely in the past, but now you can be more in tune with it, and how it works. It does take some getting used to for most people, but you have done it so many times already that it should be no problem. This will be the first day that you are back in the real world. If you can take us both somewhere, we will spend the rest of the day discussing this or whatever you like. Think of it as an incentive. Oh, and Tom, make it somewhere nice."

Tom laughed. He always thought that he had good taste. It seemed that most people were more conscious of price when it came to what they did, whereas he was more concerned with how enjoyable it would be. Sometimes it was expensive, sometimes it wasn't, but it was always perfect in the moment. He needed to clear his mind. He was thinking about all of the experiences he had in the past. Then he remembered: there is no past. There is just now. It had been a while since he had seen the outside world. Maybe they could get lunch together. That would be fun. It would be nice to see Sarah outside of this laboratory setting, and to go somewhere people didn't know him and wouldn't stare. You're getting involved again. Let the thoughts pass. Stay in the middle, balanced. Tom pictured the restaurant where he would take them. It was a cozy little place with comfortable chairs. They had the best noodles in town. The atmosphere was intimate, but not stuffy. He pictured his favorite booth and the bottle of wine they would always bring when he arrived. Tom had a relaxed smile on his face, a look of peace and serenity. When he opened his eyes, Tom was sitting in that booth next to Sarah.

"Here we are," said Sarah, "what a nice place."

"Yes. I have spent many nights sitting here alone enjoying it. I thought you might like it too. We seem to have similar tastes."

"That's expected. We are cut from the same cloth," said Sarah, giving him a smile.

The waitress walked up to the table and bowed before them. She held out the bottle of wine that Tom loved and opened it for them.

"I could get lost in this," Tom said.

"Me too. What a great way to relax."

They touched their glasses together and enjoyed everything about it. Unfortunately on that same night, there was someone there who was not enjoying what was happening as much as they were. Sam had been treating herself to dinner there and was across the dining room horrified at what she was seeing. Her mind was spinning watching Tom touch glasses next to a beautiful girl who was not her. The world was losing its color and it became hard to control her breathing. It was happening again. Tom with some other woman. How could he do this to her? She trusted him! Blind with rage, she flew over to their table without using her feet. The other diners in the restaurant, even those who were not susceptible to the energies around them, could hear an unearthly wailing howl of tortured souls screaming around them. A path was parted between Sam and the booth where Tom was sitting next to Sarah.

Tom and Sarah's attention was drawn toward Sam, as all of the warmth was drawn out of the room. Tom was oblivious as to why Sam was so upset. He was happy to see her after so long. A pleasant surprise, except for the feeling that was coming from it.

With a voice that seemed to come from an unearthly dimension, Sam addressed Tom. She was trying to use words instead of simply shrieking in his face and melting his skin away, like someone who opened the ark of the covenant, but she had completely lost control at this point.

The only words she could manage to choke out were, "do you love her?"

Tom didn't hesitate to say, "Yes, of course. She's," before Sam's eyes rolled back in her head and the fiery white light surrounded Tom completely, taking his very existence away from the restaurant. Sarah sat there staring at Sam, looking annoyed. Could she blame her? It was all ego. Sam didn't know.

"Ya just don't get it, do you?" Sarah said to Sam.

Sam started to lift her hands again, but before she could vaporize Sarah, Jack appeared in the booth in Tom's place.

"Sam, why would you do something like that?" Jack asked, taking a bite of the steak that had been brought to the table a moment before Sam had floated over angrily, "I am very disappointed." He was shaking his head as he chewed the beef tenderloin.

"So, this is Sam? Not quite what I had expected." Sarah said to Jack. He took a sip of the wine and smiled with approval.

"What are we going to do with you," Jack said to Sam, rhetorically, before teleporting away with Sarah.

Sam's anger had quickly changed into confusion because of Jack's quick cameo at the scene, as well as the question Sarah had asked before they disappeared. How did they know each other? These were answers that she would demand from Jack, but right now the situation was too hot. She had just made a big mistake, maybe not for being mad at Tom, but for disintegrating him. Why didn't Jack stop her? He could have come a moment before if he had wanted to, couldn't he? She never wanted to kill Tom, she loved him, even though he insisted on hurting her over and over again. It had all been a mistake. From every angle, though she only saw it from her own.

Sam tried to get ahold of herself. She went back to her table and slowly ate her noodles, like nothing had happened, but her mind was not on the noodles, even though it felt them. Sam had to gain control over the situation. She did her best to act like everyone in the restaurant wasn't staring at her. Everyone seemed to be in on it, but her.

Sam went about her night as she normally would, and woke up the next morning ready to try to get some answers. She sat at her breakfast table drinking orange juice and eating buttered toast with lingonberry jam while she got ready to go to work. When she got there, she went to her boss and asked for an appointment with Secret Agent Hamilton, the man who had met Tom at the bar and confirmed Jack's status with a phone call. It took some persuasion, as senior agents rarely spoke with field agents.

When she finally got to his office ten floors above, their conversation did not go the way Sam had expected.

"Good morning Agent [REDACTED], what brings you to my office?" Secret Agent Hamilton asked.

"Thank you for agreeing to see me, Sir. It is a privilege to be in your office today," Sam replied.

"You can skip the pleasantries agent, cut to the chase," said Hamilton, gesturing with his hand to wrap it up.

"Sir, I know you told me not to mention this, but I have to know more about Jack... some things have happened and I am left in the dark on the situation."

"Jack? Jack who?"

"Jack. The Cowboy, sir."

"The Cowboy? You have made contact with The Cowboy? How do you even know about him? He was disavowed from this agency years ago. Why hasn't this been in your field reports?"

"Because of the phone call, sir, you confirmed that he was an asset."

"Phone call? What phone call? I didn't make any phone calls to you."

"You mean, it wasn't you on the phone?"

"I think somebody has been playing a game with you Agent [REDACTED], this is not the kind of thing to joke about, especially with superior officers. Now you say you have made contact with The Cowboy, are you sure someone isn't playing a joke on you? Do you have any proof of what you are saying, because, frankly, I don't find this funny."

"I... I don't know."

"He is on our top most wanted list. Consider this individual to be extremely dangerous. You have to stay out of his way. We have orders on him to apprehend with extreme prejudice."

"What did he do?" Sam asked.

"That is classified. You shouldn't even know he exists. Obviously someone who has access to these files has been playing a joke on you. If you really did make contact with The Cowboy, you would already be dead. What use could you be to someone like him?"

"He didn't seem dangerous, he just wanted to help me with some kind of training."

"Really? He is training you? If you're right about this, it could be our chance to get him. I'm sure I don't have to tell you what will happen if you are wrong. If this is really the man you say it is, this could make or break your career. That whole organization has been a thorn in my side for thirty years."

"What should I do, Sir?"

"Pretend we never had this conversation. Here is my direct line if you need anything. The next time you go for 'training' we will send a team with you and raid the location. Agent, your country thanks you. Now go about your day as usual."

Sam didn't know if this was a good turn of events or not. She was still left with the same questions, now even more confused about everything. Who was Jack that he had been disavowed as an asset? Whether she knew anything or not, it was time to keep moving on and hoping for some bread crumbs.

Chapter 20
Undisclosed

After work, or during perhaps, as there was a team of agents watching her every move, Sam went to the undisclosed location where she had been training with Jack. She knocked on the door and waited, but nothing happened. She knocked again. There was the sound of the bolt sliding. The door was opened to reveal Jack's face as seen through the vertical space between him and Sam.

"You're here," Jack said, as if he was surprised. "Come in quickly. Plan Exodus. We are leaving."

Sam didn't have any time to protest. He pulled her into the building and led her down the hall to the room where they had been training. Something was different this time. Everything had been cleared out. As she walked down the hall, she noticed that all of the doors were open, and the rooms completely empty. They were abandoning this location.

"Wait," said Sam, "what is going on? I have orders to detain you."

"Detain me? Why would you want to do a thing like that?" Jack asked. He pushed aside a filing cabinet that had all the drawers open and emptied. Behind the cabinet there was a door. "We have to go. Through here is a portal, it will take us far away from the blast."

"Blast? What do you mean? You can't leave." The door opened and Adam stepped through into the now empty training room.

"It would be best if you came with us," Adam said.

"Adam? Is it really you? How are you here?" Sam asked.

"I didn't want our reintroduction to be like this, but it seems there is no choice. Do you trust me? I need you to trust me, and to listen. Jack is one of the good guys."

"I don't understand any of this, what is going on?" Sam asked.

"There will be plenty of time to explain when we go through the portal," Jack said to them.

"Alright. Fine, I'll go, but I want answers afterward," Sam said firmly.

"As you should," Jack said.

Sam listened to him and went through the portal with Adam. The door was shut behind them, leaving Jack standing in the empty room, with agents breaking their way through the front door. Jack crossed his arms and leaned against the wall. Agents dressed in black SWAT uniforms stormed through the building and surrounded Jack, who had taken the form of Sam.

Miles away, Sam and Adam appeared through a gateway of light. They were in some kind of laboratory with people standing by. The scene they had just left was being watched on monitors all around them.

"Why didn't he come with us?" Sam asked.

"He couldn't," said Adam, "if he did they may have reopened the portal and followed. They are not after us, they just want him.

They watched the screen as agents stormed the building in search of Jack.

"How is he..." Sam started.

"He can take any form," Adam replied. They watched as the Sam who was really Jack held up his hands and started to talk.

"I'm an agent, the target escaped."

The team lowered their weapons and waited for a response from their superior officers, which came in the form of Secret Agent Hamilton, who walked up to Sam and looked her over. He put his face within an inch and stared into Sam's eyes.

"You think you can fool me with that act, Jack? Still up to the same old tricks, huh?" said Hamilton.

The new Sam changed back into Jack, causing the other soldiers to raise their weapons in surprise.

"Long time no see, Hamilton. Why *did* you leave the company anyway? You are one of us."

"Oh, Jack, what am I going to do with you? Always the odd man out," said Hamilton.

"I could leave here right now."

"But you know we would follow you. We always do. We always track you down. Why did you have to kill so many agents last time? I might have been able to get you off with a warning."

"They didn't understand. We just want to live peacefully. The advancements we are making to our very existence are far more advanced than all of the scientific experiments regular people are performing combined."

"I know, Jack. You can't keep hiding it from us. Don't you know what we could do with that kind of technology? Why not use it to help your country?"

"Big countries are run by small men. Tiny petty tyrants. They are short-sighted. We want to use these powers to improve and build upon mankind, not tear it down. We want to end wars and starvation, not make money. The government is comprised of selfish little men who want more and more money that they won't be able to take with them when it's over. Don't they realize they are going to die? They think money is more valuable than people. Human lives. If we can't help our fellow man, we might as well be animals."

"Turn it off," said Adam, "I can't watch this."

The screen turned black as the feed was disconnected.

"Why didn't the See-ers see this?" Adam demanded of them.

"Who says they didn't," said Sarah, walking into the room.

"Why would we let him get captured?" asked Adam.

"It's all part of a bigger plan. We needed Sam. He wants us to continue training her the way we have been training you."

"Adam! What is she doing here?" Sam demanded of him, referring to Sarah. The last time Sam had seen this girl was at the dinner table with the love of her life.

"It's about time we tell her," Sarah said.

"Yes," said Adam, "I agree. Sam, it seems they have been keeping you in the dark. All for good reason, I'm sure."

"I'll be the judge of that," Sam said.

"About a month ago, I woke up from my coma. I didn't want to tell anyone until I could take care of myself. I didn't want to be a burden on anyone, and after having laid there for so long, my body was not ready to take on everyday life. It is quite common for coma patients to undergo years of physical therapy before they are able to resume their old lives. On the second day I was awake, Sarah came to me and told me there was a better way. She said that in times of great stress, such as the car accident, certain energies are awakened in our bodies that allow us to do extraordinary things. By tapping in to that source, I was able to reduce my therapy down to a very short amount of time. Afterward, I continued working with my energy field to access the powers that were awakened. I am a student here."

"Where is here?" asked Sam.

"The Shadow Corporation," Sarah interrupted, "we are a group dedicated to understanding and unlocking the human potential. We have many faces and branches, including physical therapy. You already know Jack, and of course, Tom. They are all part of it."

"So you were..." Sam started.

"Yes," Sarah said, "I was helping Tom to access his powers."

"But dinner... it seemed so clear what was happening. He said that he loves you."

"He does, but you didn't give him a chance to explain. He has been here with us training since he left you. We told him not to say anything about the corporation because we don't need anybody else poking around here, especially someone with government credentials. In time, we would have told you everything, but it was too soon, especially with Jack training you, and then there was the incident at the restaurant."

"But, I saw how he was looking at you..." Sam said, pleading for some small chance of being justified for her action.

"He was celebrating the next benchmark in his training. Tom is getting his connection back. You are still not seeing the truth. Sam. Tom is my brother. I am his sister! That is why he loves me. I'm not a threat to your precious ego," Said Sarah.

"What? Tom never said anything about a sister," Sam objected.

"That's because he didn't know. There was no way to be a part of his life without him worrying that he created me, until he lost his powers. During his training he realized who I was and yes, we are close. He loves me, but not like that."

Oops. This was all too much for Sam. She suddenly had a sick feeling in her stomach.

"I need to lay down," Sam said.

"Adam, please show her to her room," said Sarah.

Adam helped her to the room they had prepared.

"It will be okay," he said, "they filled me in on everything I missed while I was sleeping. I saw what happened with Tom. It wasn't your fault. You can't blame yourself for it. We have to listen to these people, they can help us. I trust them and I know this might not be the right time to mention this, but there is something between Sarah and I."

"What?" Sam said. "You can't keep springing things on me like this. I didn't even know Tom had a sister, and now you are dating her? Adam, I killed Tom. This is not okay, how is it going to be all right?"

"I know Tom. If anyone can come back from whatever happened, it is him," Adam said.

"But you don't understand, he lost his powers. He isn't the same Tom you knew. Even if he was training here, he couldn't possibly have survived."

"I'm sorry. We may never know what happened to Tom, but we have other work that needs to be done in the meantime. We need to keep training so we can rescue Jack. Your resources with the bureau will be valuable to us, but we have to act fast before they take away your security clearance. Sarah told me they would escalate the intensity of the training to get us where we need to be for something so extreme. I know you can do it, I saw your training sessions with Jack."

"It's just so much to take in," Sam said, "you were watching me? I don't want to do anything right now, my mind is so clouded."

"That's enough for now," Sarah said over the comms system, "let her rest."

Adam left the room and Sam laid down in the bed trying to grasp everything that happened.

Sarah had been training Tom? She was his sister? Adam is out of the coma? He is here training? Jack is involved with all of it? Her life had just been turned upside down.

Chapter 21
Jack of all Trades

To understand all that happened next, we need to understand who this Jack fellow is. His whole life has been a mystery up until this point to everyone reading the story, as well as the main participants. Everyone except for Sarah, of course, who heard the stories while working with him at the Shadow Corporation. He was a rogue, a renegade, a man of many actions, but this great hero, like Tom, had a rough start, as most of us do.

As a young boy, Jack would frequently get into trouble. He was sent to military school by his parents, who didn't know how to deal with his antics. He was a boy like most children, but quite different, indeed. From a young age, he was in touch with his energy field. He could do anything he put his mind to, if he so wished.

The one major difference for Jack, was that he could take upon the appearance of others. Even though he was a small child, he could mimic the statue of a grown man. Jack had even turned into the family dog one day which was quite upsetting to the veterinarian, who didn't think dogs could talk up to that point.

As Jack grew older, he started to understand discipline, and finally found a roll he could fill in society. The exercise program at the school turned him into a solid figure who would be intimidating to most of us normal bodied beings. He excelled at everything he did, even by his own merit, not just with his connection to the energy field. Tom wished me to include that last sentence, so that we do not soil his reputation. We need not overlook that Jack was a very smart and well-abled man.

He served in the army for a short time, before he was kicked out for imitating commanding officers one too many times. For Jack, that wasn't just pretending, it was becoming. As far as anyone was concerned, he was that person. The others around him were not amused, they did not know what to do with such a person, high marks or not. They would probably capture and experiment on him if he wasn't already cooperating with the system. That, and he could disappear any time by becoming someone else. It would be impossible and unnecessary to put him behind bars, and he was much more valuable as an asset.

Jack lived a semi-normal life after he was discharged. He changed his appearance many times, to avoid anyone who might be interested in pursuing him, and worked on his hobbies as he went from job to job. Then he fell in love. He had been working at a small restaurant as a server, a form of actor, as he called it. The girl he liked became a regular at the restaurant so that she could spend more time with him.

Any girl would be attracted to Jack for his looks, but she saw something deeper in him. She admired that he wasn't tied down to anything. He was unattached and easy going. When something bad happened, he would be the first one to smile and find a way to work through it. That kind of turn-around was next to invisible in everyone else. Other people got so involved with every little thing and would argue about it and dwell on who to blame. Not Jack. He understood what life was really about, and what is important. They had a son together and everything seemed perfect. They named him after his father, Thomas Michael Livingston. Their son demanded special attention, as he seemed to exhibit similar tendencies as Jack, when it came to controlling various energies. They were a happy family until a year later when Jack's wife had another baby. A girl this time. They named her Sarah, and she had the same potential as the first. Sarah and Tom, working together, were too much for Jack and his wife to handle. They decided it would be better if they split up and took care of each of the children individually. The combined energy of the two was too much for anyone to handle, even with Jack being connected to the energy field. These children needed special attention, that they would only get from a full time parent. Jack left with Sarah and Tom's mother stayed with him. She met a man later, who Tom would believe to have been his father, but you already know how that story goes.

Jack and Sarah were inseparable. He was an ideal father. He was protective of her, though he need not be, given the things she could do. He was more worried that people would find out she was different and persecute her for it. It was not easy to be a child who was different. Jack wanted her to be comfortable for who she was, not to be judged by people who didn't understand. With his military background and the attention he had been given in the past, he applied to work for the government. They selected him for a special program that had just been started to investigate the universal energy field and manipulation. If he had top level clearance, he would be able to make sure his daughter was properly looked after and kept safe from people who would inevitably be afraid of her. His new job would allow him to pay for the top schools that would treat her right.

Research was being performed in the field of... well let's just say 'special' Special Agents. The government had seen things they couldn't understand, all around the world, and knew that the next generation of soldier would be people like Jack who could do these extraordinary things. If people like this existed, they would have to be on the same side as they were, if they wished to live in peace. These people were afraid of these special beings who had a deeper connection with reality. Fortunately for them, Jack was on their side from the start, as he had been trained at their own institutions.

Jack was given a high level position at the bureau and his very existence was only known by those at the top. The things he could do were valuable to national security and they had to be kept secret. He was working alongside Mike Hamilton, who was a new addition to the bureau. They had a lot in common. Not just their abilities, but their beliefs of how they should be used, and with what consideration. Jack and Mike rose up in ranks and started to shape things the way they wanted them. People with special abilities would no longer be persecuted.

Then came the incident. A group of bigots captured a boy with special abilities. A week later, the boy was found dead. It was a sad day for Jack and Mike, who had been fighting so hard for integration, but one of great change for Todd Deckard, their fellow special Special Agent. Todd didn't support their point of view on the situation. For him it was a slippery slope of their kind being killed because of their differences. It had been done so many times in history.

"They killed an innocent child because they believed he had powers, what more has to happen before you are willing to do something?" Todd demanded, standing up for what he believed in.

"Now is not the time to act," said Mike, "if we start a war, countless more lives will be lost on both sides. We need to resolve this peacefully."

"We were resolving it peacefully, and look what happened! They killed him in cold blood. A child! What if that had been your child? Jack? You don't seem to have a lot to say."

"Don't bring my family into this. I can understand both sides. There is no telling what I would do if this hatred came into my life directly, but it is a small group of people who are doing the hating. They are scared and reacting out of fear. They are cowards to do such a thing, especially to a child. I do not support violence, even if it is in opposition to violence. There is no need to start a war. We have the power to investigate and put these people behind bars. That is where we need to start," Jack said.

"Jack, you know how the system works," Todd protested, "they'll get away with it. Even if they do serve time, what is it compared to that boy's life? They killed him. That could have been any one of us out there, kidnapped and tortured. How can you stand by and let them get away with it?" Deckard demanded.

"I'm not letting them get away with anything. We have the upper hand. With our powers and the resources of the bureau, we can take in all of them and make them understand."

"Make them understand? They don't need to understand anything, they need to be punished. Do you think you can do that when the time comes? Do you think you have what it takes to change their minds? These are cruel, horrible people, and you want to let them get away with their crimes."

"The world isn't ready for us yet. We have to keep our existence a secret, everyone like us. We have to identify them and keep them safe," said Jack.

"To protect them? Like we did the boy? How do you think we'll be able to do that? Especially when their name is on a list. That just makes it more likely that someone will find it and take advantage," said Deckard.

"I have been thinking about it for a long time. I have a way, but it will take time. I will take it upon myself to make sure only the right people are in on it."

"We don't have time! They are killing our children on the streets! I won't stand by and wait for action."

Deckard didn't show up for work again after that. The next time they heard of him, was a few weeks later on the news. He was the lead suspect in the disappearance of the bigots who had gotten away with the murder of the boy. Deckard had found them and served his idea of justice. Afterward, he started a faction, of people with abilities, who would take the law into their own hands. Jack and Mike didn't support what he was doing, but they didn't stop him either.

Jack was working on a solution for protecting and training young people with abilities, when he was approached by a tall man with dark hair and a goatee. He said his name was Howard, and that he had all the required resources for Jack and Mike to start what would be known as: The Shadow Corporation. Over the next few years everything was put into place and the training facility was operational. Howard gave Jack guidance for instructing students, along with techniques for using the energy. It manifested differently in everyone, but these were the things that were attainable, given practice. The process would be different for everyone.

The Shadow Corporation grew larger and larger, making advancements in science and biology well beyond what Howard had given. They could detect the potential for field manipulation before children with abilities were even born. Everything worked like a well-oiled machine, the entire universe. If they followed the bread crumbs, they could know everything, and find the key to existence itself.

Jack knew that people weren't ready for it yet. They could not force people who were not ready into the program, or to embrace their powers. It would be rejected by the host. Their detection system followed people with abilities until they found a time that was deemed appropriate to free them. They had it down to an exact science. When someone was ready, the Corporation would come into their life and show them the truth. They would open their minds and train them. Sarah was among the first group of students at the facility. She was among the few who started at a young age, thanks to Jack, and cultivated her awareness of the energy field, instead of being afraid of it. Jack finally gave her formal training at the facility, because of their relationship. They both grew to be the strongest and most in tune of the people there.

Knowing the risk of being exposed to the world, they kept their work very secretive. Not even the bureau knew about this new organization, but one day that changed. There was an investigation into what this corporation was and who was behind it. Jack and Mike did everything they could to suppress intel until it came down to an ultimatum. One of them would have to be linked to it and the other would stay in the bureau as an inside source. It was decided that Jack would take the fall, because he wanted to be able to spend time with his daughter at the corporation. The agent who stayed at the bureau would have to keep his distance from everything related to the corporation, or risk being exiled as well.

The terrorist group, led by Deckard, continued to execute elitists who thought that people with abilities were a threat to the country. It was ironic, in a way, that he was proving them right. Mike continued to investigate the faction, as well as the Shadow Corporation, but nothing ever seemed to be conclusive. He was suppressing just enough to keep them from being caught, while holding his cover.

The Shadow Corporation kept track of Tom, Sam, and Adam. They watched from a distance, as Jack wanted to know that his son was safe, even though he couldn't risk meeting him. Mike escorted Sam into the agency so that they could set things up to their advantage. The bureau already knew about Tom, and kept him on their watch list. When Tom lost his powers, special agent Mike Hamilton made confirmation by meeting Tom at the bar, pretending he didn't know anything. Opportunity knocked, and everything was set in place so that Sarah would meet Tom and train him to bring back his abilities. They kept Sam in the dark about it as long as they could, so that they would be able to put her into an intense situation where she would have to rescue Jack. He believed that any extreme emotional experience would bring about an awakening of inert energies in Sam. Their training had been going well, but then she blew the whistle and went to Agent Hamilton about him. They had to expedite their plan and make it look like Jack had been captured. This is where we resume our story.

Chapter 22
Saving The Cowboy

"Have they stopped listening yet?" Hamilton asked, "I couldn't have lasted another minute without laughing. I think they bought it. I told her not to ask questions about your past."

"Yeah, they've stopped listening. It's a shame we had to speed things up like this. Sam has been making so much progress, but we can't have her asking questions to the wrong people."

"You're sure she's going to rescue you?"

"Of course. Sarah has it all in place at the corporation. They are going to finish her training and then send her on a rescue mission for me."

"You know, I can't believe how long it has been since I've seen you Jackie boy."

"It has been a long time. That is the price of security. Thank you for keeping an eye on Tom. The way he uses his powers, I worry about him being seen by the wrong people. I know he could have stopped them, but what if he didn't see it coming?"

"Jack, that's what family does. We are here for each other. Tom is a good kid. He continues to make the right decisions and has managed to stay off of Deckard's radar. You should be proud of him."

"I am. I'm proud of both of my children. I only wish I could have been there for Tom when he needed a father. The extra life lessons that are needed for people with these abilities comes at a high price, and can only be taught by those who have experience with them."

"Alright," said Hamilton, clapping his hands together, "let's get this set up."

Jack put his hands out to be cuffed.

"Remember, we have to make this look real," he said.

Hamilton cuffed Jack and said to him, "Back into character. We can make it look real, but we also have to make it believable."

He led Jack out of the building where the other agents had been waiting for his command. They took him into the back of a van and blindfolded him on the way to the prison.

"I thought you would like this one," Hamilton said, pushing Jack into a jail cell, "it is the same one we had your son in." Jack knew he wasn't really being held prisoner, but he played along.

"What are you doing, Jack?" came a voice from behind him, in the cell that was fit for a king. Tom had left everything behind: the books, the furniture, all of the comforts and luxuries that were not part of any other cell. Somehow it took up the space of a living room, even though it had been the same size as the other cells, before Tom had been held prisoner. Jack spun around to see who it was that awaited him in the cell. It was none other than Todd Deckard himself, sitting calmly in the lion's den.

"Why are you letting them keep you here?" Deckard asked him, "You see what I mean? You were their top agent and now you are their prisoner. That is what they do. They persecute. They are afraid of anyone they can't control so they try to destroy what they don't understand instead of embracing evolution."

"It's not what it looks like. You still assume the worst Deckard," Jack replied. Maybe they had been a little too convincing.

"You are going to tell me that you are here by choice? I know you Jack. You are a smart guy. Why would I ever believe that you chose to be here. Especially after Hamilton betrayed our cause," said Deckard.

"It wasn't Hamilton. He is still working with me and the corporation. It's an act. A show. We are pulling the strings so that our students will grow stronger."

"Training your students by lying to them? That doesn't sound like you. How are you going to do anything from here? Now *my* group, we've got it all planned out. That's why I'm here. I wanted to warn you to keep your loved ones away from your facility when the bomb goes off."

"What? What are you talking about? Is that supposed to be some kind of metaphor?" asked Jack.

"No. The building is going to be destroyed, taking countless lives of special individuals like you and me. It is going to be linked to the government. Just what we need to spur the revolution. People will protest and we will be able to retaliate tenfold without any objection. If they see their government killing innocent people, they will become sympathetic to the cause. People will buy into the mass panic and we will be able to kill everyone who is against us and get away with it scot-free. Just like any war we start with other countries. Make it look like they attacked first."

"At the cost of my students? People like us?"

"Collateral damage. Everything comes at a price, Jack. You should know that by now. Even having a second child, it tore apart your family. There is always a cost."

"I love my family."

"I bet you would have loved to keep your family together too, but because we are looked down upon as outsiders, that wasn't allowed to happen. There was no way to protect your family and still keep it together. You know what it was like. How can you wish that upon future generations instead of creating a better world for them?" Deckard asked.

"I won't let you do this. You can't use people for your own means, they are not play things you can just toss around at a whim."

"It's not your choice anymore. You're here in jail. I came here out of a sense of kinship. We are family. I care about you and your kids. Nobody knows as much about this as you and me. I want you to know that it is not personal, but we have to speed up the revolution. I can't stand by idly while this continues."

"You can't do this. Those are my people at the corporation, not yours. My family, my friends, people I promised a better life."

"It is already done, and they will have a better life. The ones who survive, at least. It will be a better world for them when we take over." Todd disappeared from the cell. Jack ran over to the bars of the cell and started yelling, "Mike! Mike! MIKE!"

Chapter 23
A Place Between Places

The white light that surrounded Tom was now all around him in every direction. It was a familiar place, with nothing but white. As he appeared there with singed clothing, he finished his sentence, not realizing that he was no longer in the restaurant, "my sister." With no alternative after looking at his surroundings, Tom started to walk. He couldn't help but laugh to himself at what had happened. It had been an innocent dinner, but he could understand how it looked to Sam, especially with the history they had. He wasn't upset with her at all, in fact he was quite amused. It was nice to see that her powers were getting as strong as his, and that she was willing to stand up for herself. Tom always liked that Sam was strong. He felt that she could deal with almost anything that came her way. So Tom kept walking, laughing to himself, and picturing the situation over and over in his head, when he came upon a chair. It was an all-white chair. He almost missed it because everything was white here, but in a world of nothingness, even the smallest abnormality would be detectable. It was a strange place, there were no shadows. That meant the light wasn't coming from a specific direction. It seemed to be everywhere.

Tom took his que and sat down in the chair. There was nothing to see. A very interesting place, indeed. He somehow knew that he wouldn't be able to teleport out of here. Slowly, a figure appeared in the distance, getting closer and closer, until there was a man standing right in front of him.

"You look familiar," Tom said.

"Hey buddy, I didn't think I would be seeing you again so soon. It's me, John," the man said.

"It is? You look different," said Tom.

"I know. In this place we are not really occupying our bodies in the same way we were before. This is a place in between places. The visual identification of ourselves here is just mental. It is something that is created based on how we think we look. A spirit body, if you will. I sensed you were in danger so I came out here to help you. What happened?"

"I think Sam may have overreacted."

"Ha! A bit, it seems, what did you do to make her so angry?"

"She caught me having dinner with another girl."

"Ouch. I thought you were done with that kind of thing."

"I am. She didn't let me explain that it was my sister," said Tom.

"Ohhhhh, you have a sister? How come we've never met? Which reminds me, you have to meet my wife. She is incredible. You would love the conversations we have."

"I just found out she was my sister. She has been helping me train to get my powers back."

"Yes! I heard you lost your powers and that Bhagwan left his body. I hope you are dealing with it well, I know how much he meant to you. I had someone who helped me along the path too, and it was hard losing him."

"It's all right, he is still with me, as long as I keep him in my heart."

"That is the right way to look at it. I was shocked when I found out your father was involved too! What a twist!" John said, nodding his head.

"My father? I think you have that wrong. My father is dead," Tom replied, mater-of-factly.

"Oh. I've said too much. I thought you were farther along in the story. Sometimes I lose track of the script, time being all the same thing to me and all... So, I didn't come here to talk to you all day, but it was nice to catch up. Let's get this over with. A lot more time has already passed on your plane, so we need to send you back fairly quickly," said John.

"Wait, what were you talking about with my father?"

"Fantastic, here we go, APERTAM..." Zhuuuum. The light changed and Tom was shot back into the realm of the living material bodies, and found himself back in his own. He patted himself down, remembering now what it was like to be inside of this meat-husk. Very confining. He could see the energy field around his own body. It was beautiful. His hands interacted with it, little molecules being left over when he touched everything. There was a trail in the air as he waved his hand. His mind was still partially set to the other world. It grew brighter when he smiled and laughed at how cool it was. This vision of his own energy field started to fade into a veil that was clouded by the mind. If he concentrated he could barely see the outline of it around his hands, but it had been blocked once again, just like it is for most people.

"Neat," Tom said to himself. He looked around to see where he was. It was the bedroom with the broken two-way mirror for a window. The room he had been staying in at the Shadow Corporation. He remembered the night he had broken down and how his sister Sarah had been there to comfort him in that time of strife. No time for reminiscing. Tom felt different now, after that experience with John. He was ready to face his problems head on. He opened the door and took a step out.

Chapter 24
Up in Smoke

Sarah ran down the hall to the room where Sam was, and caught hold of Adam on the way.

"Adam, the See-ers saw something!" she yelled at him.

"Isn't that what they are supposed to do?" Adam asked, not getting the severity of what had been foreseen.

"We have to evacuate the building. They have predicted something terrible, but we have to keep it quiet to prevent panic. Help me get everyone out of the building."

Sam sensed something and walked out of the room into the hallway.

"We have to evacuate the building," Adam said to her, "there is something going on."

Jack materialized in the hallway in front of all of them.

"You have to get everyone out, there is a bomb," he said to them.

"Jack?" they all said in unison.

"No time to explain, we have to get everyone out."

Then, to further complicate things, Tom stepped out of his room, which was only a few doors down from Sam's room and saw them all in the hallway.

"Sam!" Tom said.

"Tom?" they all said together.

Tom's mind had been clear and still while he was in the other world. He had taken that feeling back with him and could see this world as an outsider once again. It all made sense.

"Dad," said Tom to Jack, "I can see it."

"What do you mean, Dad?" asked Sam, "Jack is your father?"

"Yes," said Sarah, to confirm what Tom had said, "Jack is our father."

"Adam?" said Tom.

"Adam," said Sam, "he woke up."

"It worked! That's fantastic! I'm so glad he is okay," said Tom.

Everyone was smiling and nodding, but then Jack interrupted them.

"We don't have time for this," Jack said, "there is going to be an…" BOOM. The building shook around them as the left side of the hallway was blown into the middle a few feet away from them. There was a bright flash. Alarms started going off around the building. There was smoke and rubble all around and everyone was pulling themselves up off the floor, having been thrown down by the blast. The alarms were dull in the background of their hearing, in the forefront was a high pitched ringing. Tom could hear them all yelling around him.

"WHAT?" yelled Adam.

"WE HAVE TO GET OUT OF THE BUILDING," Jack said using his hands to emphasize what he was saying as if everyone could understand him, just by looking at his hands. They already knew they needed to get out.

There were sirens and horns sounding in the distance, coming for the now burning building. Everything was shaking around them, and they didn't know how much longer the building would hold. Then there was a second explosion, it started to come through the wall in slow motion, fire shooting down the hall toward them, but it froze. Tom stood there holding his hand out. He had stopped time around them.

"We have to get everyone out!" Jack yelled, but in this new silence, his voice thundered into their ears. All of the noise and alarm around them had stopped in this state of suspended time.

Everyone was tense. Sam slowly stood up and brushed her hair back. There was blood on her hand. She looked at her hand as if she hadn't seen it before, confused by the blood. Something had hit her during the first explosion, but she would be all right. They were all disoriented, except for Tom. He had already seen it happen.

"Tom!" she yelled. She ran over to him and hugged him like her life depended on it. The fact that he was still alive had just sunk in. She hadn't killed him.

Now was no time to say anything about what had happened between them or discuss how she had reacted. There was pure love between them now, when everything else had fallen silent. Her mind was still.

The five of them went through the building clearing out the frozen people who had not been part of the time-bubble. They didn't have any weight to them. It was like carrying feathers out of the building as they took them one by one, but there were some who had been too close to the initial explosion. They couldn't be saved. They were like sad puppets, with no life left in their eyes, but they were carried out anyway.

When they were outside of the building with the other students, staff, and lifeless bodies, they looked up at the building, witnessing the smoke that was frozen in the sky and the fire that had shot out of the windows and froze. It was a horrible photograph that left them speechless. There were news van's that had been pulling up and firemen with hoses running toward the building. The entire scene was more than hectic, but in this state of frozen time it had an eerie peacefulness. A feeling that everything would be okay.

"How did this happen? Who would do this?" Sarah asked, speaking to everyone who was left, still trying to believe what had happened. The only sound to be heard was their own heavy breathing, and their confused questions about what was going on.

Jack put his hand up to his head and rubbed his temple with his thumb and forefinger. It was gruesome. He didn't make it in time to save everyone.

A quiet noise grew louder and louder as it came closer to them. Everything started to move again, slowly at first, speeding up into real time. The sirens were back, the screaming, the noise, the confusion.

"Everyone is out!" Jack yelled at the firemen, keeping them from entering the building. The ground shook as there was another explosion.

The black vans from the bureau were pulling up to the situation to suppress what had happened and to clear out the now defunct headquarters of the Shadow Corporation. All of their data had been backed up in a secure location. They would be able to rebuild.

"GET BACK, GET BACK!" yelled the firemen to the crowd, "IT'S COMING DOWN!"

Everyone watching shielded their eyes as they turned around to see the great sight. The entire street would soon be covered in grey smoke for four blocks around as the building lost its hold and came crashing down into itself with a roar. It happened in slow motion to everyone around who was watching it, this state of panic had made them all experience what Tom's group had just felt in the moment of time coming back to normal speed. A sick feeling found it's home in all of them as they tried to believe what they were seeing.

Then they couldn't see anything through the smoke. All around were sirens, people screaming, babies crying, people of authority yelling commands.

As the smoke cleared, the camera crew wiped off the lens of the camera. People shook their heads like a dog coming in from the rain in order to shake off the dust. Everything was covered in grey, like some kind of unclean snow had fallen on them. The emergency crews were trying to save everyone who had been injured in the building. Debris had flown everywhere and hit some people on the way down.

"We are here at the sight of a national tragedy," the female reporter started to say to the camera after dusting herself off, "as countless lives were lost in this tragic event." She put her hand to her ear as instructions came in from the station. "I am getting news now that the building was not up to code. They had been having problems with their gas lines for some time, a repairman was on his way to analyze what was needed, when an unknown source ignited the gas. The severity of the leaks had not been determined, but as you can see, even a small leak can lead to a major disaster. We have lost one of the biggest and oldest buildings right in the heart of downtown..."

"A GAS LEAK!" Todd shouted at his television, "THEY'RE CALLING IT A GAS LEAK!?! That doesn't change anything! We can't retaliate to a gas leak, it was supposed to be fanatics! Now we will look like the bad guys! We have to act. We are going to retaliate, whether the people are on our side or not. It was for nothing. We lost our own soldiers for nothing. Nothing has changed, it didn't work. How could it not work. IT WAS FOR NOTHING!" He threw his hands at the television and blew it to pieces all around the room. He stood there breathing heavy for a moment, regaining his composure. Then he took out his phone, put in the number, and held it to his ear.

"Yes. No, it didn't work. I know," he said to whomever was on the line, "we have to go ahead with our plans, anyway. Move them up. We have to act now. No, I don't think we need plan B just yet. I'll be damned if they think the next one is a gas leak. We will have our day."

To everyone who hadn't destroyed their television, and had left it on the same channel, they saw the scene put into a small box in the corner as the main screen showed an important looking man walking to a podium to address the nation.

"People of this great nation. We have in front of us one of the biggest disasters that has occurred in the past decade. I want you to know that we will stand together as a country. We will do everything it takes to prevent this from ever happening again. I have already rushed an act through congress to install greater protection and safety checks for all gas lines in public buildings. We will not let atrocities like this occur in this great nation, out of negligence. I want you to know that as your leader, I will see to it personally that those responsible for the regulation of this building will be put through much more intensive training to prevent anything like this from ever happening again. I would like to ask you for a moment of silence for the people we lost in this tragic accident. … … … … May God be with the souls we lost today and their families. As your leader, I want everyone to know that they live in a country where they can always feel safe. It is our duty to protect the people. We will not stand by idly when threats like this are pervasive throughout our own homes."

"What are they saying happened?" Jack asked them, as if they could hear any better than he could.

"I think they're calling it a gas leak," said Adam.

"A gas leak? Ha. Ha ha ha." Jack looked up at the sky and shook his head as tears started to come to his eyes because of the waste of life he had just witnessed. "He thought they would report it for what it was, but they covered it up. It was all for nothing."

"What are you talking about?" asked Adam.

"Deckard. Todd Deckard. He leads a faction of people with abilities who promote violence against the norm. He did this. He wanted to create a reason for retaliation, so that the people would be on our side, but the whole thing has been defused with this excuse for what happened," Jack explained.

"So his plans have been stopped?"

"...no. I don't think so. People like Deckard don't take failure as an option. He's going to keep trying, and we need to stop him."

"Where do we begin?" Sam asked.

"We have to regroup. Get everyone together, to our next safe location."

"Where is that?" Sam asked.

"You know where it is. The training facility," Jack replied.

"But they know about it, they raided it, everything was cleared out. Won't that be the first place they look?"

"This isn't going to make sense, but Hamilton is on our side. What happened was just an act. He and I are old buddies. We worked together in the bureau and started the Shadow Corporation together. He is one of us. He has abilities too, but has been hiding it so that we had a man on the inside."

"This doesn't make any sense, I saw you. You were taken to prison."

"It was all an act. I'll explain everything later. Our plans changed, and I had to come here to warn everyone. Give our people the coordinates to the safe house and we'll regroup there. I can't risk being seen here." Jack closed his eyes and disappeared from the site. The four of them went around trying to find everyone who had been in the building and gave them the coordinates. Sam didn't know if the safe house could fit so many people, but comfortable or not, they had to get to safety. When they found everyone, they gathered in a circle and disappeared together. The core group ended up at Tom's house. No one would look for them there.

"What just happened?" Sarah asked.

"We were attacked," said Sam.

"I know that," said Sarah, "but why? It didn't mean anything. How could we let this happen. I knew everyone there. The people who died... they were my friends. I helped train them. I recruited them. They wouldn't have been there if..."

"Stop," Adam said, "stop blaming yourself. No one could have predicted this. We are good people, how would we know that our own kind would do something like this?"

"The corporation... it was formed to keep things like this from happening. It was meant to protect them from intolerance, how could people like us do this?"

"It's horrible," Adam said. Tom closed his eyes and swallowed a hard swallow that was partially made of the dust that they had all been breathing at the scene of their old headquarters collapsing. He shook his head slowly, trying to wake up from this. He had seen and done many things with his powers but had never dealt with this kind of thing. The horror. The hatred. The loss of life. All a waste. How does one continue on after this?

"We have to make sure that nothing like this can ever happen again," Tom said. "We have been so wrapped up in our own problems that we forgot to watch the world around us. There is so much more. It's not just about us. We are not the only ones in the world. There are good people, and bad people. We were too wrapped up in our own feelings for each other to see what was right in front of us and we let it into our home."

"Stop," Sarah said, starting to cry, "just stop. We couldn't have known. It's not the time. I can't do this. I knew those people. They were my life. I don't want to hear any of it. I don't want to be a part of it anymore."

Adam held her against him as she cried into his chest. Tom wanted to give them words of encouragement, so they could move on and continue what they were doing. He wanted to stop the people who were responsible for this, but it was too soon. There was too much happening, too much sorrow, too much grief, and too much loss to think about anything but how much it hurt.

Chapter 25
Picking up the Pieces

"Tom, we need to talk," Sam said. They were still recovering from what happened at Shadow Corporation, but there was still an elephant in the room. For all intents and purposes, Sam had pretty much killed Tom when she found him at the restaurant with Sarah, not knowing it was his sister.

"Sure," Tom said, "let's go to the bedroom away from everyone else."

She followed him to the bedroom and closed the door. Tom sat down on the bed. Sam leaned against the door for a minute thinking about how to get started.

"I'm sorry for what I did to you, Tom," Sam said, "phew, I have been holding that in for so long now."

Tom laughed and patted the space next to him for her to come sit down.

"It was an honest mistake," he said, "though I do wish you would have talked to me first."

"It is a very sensitive subject for me. Seeing you there with Sarah made me feel like it was happening all over again, like I was losing you. I can't tell you how much that hurt."

"I didn't mean to scare you. I didn't know you would be there. They told me to keep everything secret, or I would have loved to have you join us for dinner. When I found out she was my sister, it changed things for me. I always thought I was alone, beside my mother, and I never felt like she could understand me the way a sibling would. I was going to tell you everything when they let me back out into the world."

"I understand, it's just that it felt so real... it was such a shock to me... I mean the first time... you never even said you were sorry," said Sam.

"Do you want me to apologize?"

"Only if you really mean it. Not just because I want you to."

"I'm sorry. Of course I'm sorry. I have regretted it since the moment it happened. We were in such a bad place after the accident. We should have talked to each other but we just internalized everything. I only did it because I felt like I had already lost you and I'm willing now to do whatever it takes to make this work," Tom said.

"I am too. We both made mistakes. I love you. I would do anything for you too. I think that's our blessing and our curse, that we love each other. I was so upset that you can do so much, but didn't save Adam. He was asleep for so long while you just stood there knowing you could help him at any time."

"Is that what you thought happened?"

"It was, how do you explain it? I went back to the memory and saw you doing something to him right before the crash. You could have saved him. What were you doing?"

"I was saving him. Adam was supposed to die in that crash. I transferred enough energy to him to keep him alive, but he had to stay in a coma until the right time or the universe would take him again. Every time I have saved someone's life, they have died anyway within a few days. I knew with Adam that the only chance I had was to keep him under the radar. I used my energy to keep him alive, but not enough so that the universe would notice or be influenced by his survival. I always hoped there would be a time when he could come back to his life. Now that he has been awake for so long, I know that he is going to be okay."

"Why didn't you just tell me that in the first place?" asked Sam.

"I didn't know if it would work. I hoped it would, but if it didn't, then it would be my fault that he died. That wouldn't be something we could come back from. We have too much history together, all three of us, to deal with his death being associated with me. That's one thing I can't do. I can't save lives. We got lucky this time, with Adam, but it is not something I have power over. I'm sorry I didn't tell you sooner. I was waiting to see if he could ever wake up."

"I thought you could do anything," Sam told him.

"It's not as simple as that. Some things are arranged by the universe. Those are the only things that have to happen in a predetermined fashion, the way that they are meant to."

"I just hope we can put the past behind us."

"No, the past is what makes us who we are. It is the strength behind our love. That we made it through those times shows us that we can do anything together."

"So you still want to be with me? Even after I killed you?" she asked.

"Yes, and you, after I cheated on you?"

"As long as you promise it will never happen again."

"Yes, but the same goes for you." Tom winked and kissed her. They were starting to get closer to each other when the door opened.

"What, do you live in a model home, Tom? Everything is nice on the outside and empty on the inside. I went through all the cabinets," Adam said to them from the doorway.

"The coffee is real," said Tom.

"Yeah, you two love birds don't need to add caffeine to this situation," Adam replied.

"It's time to get going anyway," said Sam, "we have to meet Jack and the survivors. Has Sarah calmed down?"

"She's getting there," said Adam, "should one of us stay behind? I mean, in case the location is compromised. It would be good to have backup on the outside."

"No," Sam said, "we need all the manpower we can get there. Someone here would be a waste of resources. They would be a sitting duck. Strength in numbers. We all go together."

They gathered everything, including their composure, and continued on to the safe location, where Jack and the others were waiting. Upon arrival, they were rushed into the building to a lecture that Jack was giving. He was recapitulating what happened, who was behind it, and how they should proceed. The newcomers sat and listened. They heard all about Deckard, and how he had started the faction to fight against intolerance, in the name of justice. Tom could understand how the man felt. It would have been easy to be on either side and to feel right about it. Even a wise man acts under the impulse of his own nature: all beings follow nature. Of what use is restraint? It is only a question of morality, if you believe in that sort of thing.

Tom closed his eyes with a sick feeling in his stomach about what had happened and what was to come. He felt his body getting lighter. He had often felt this way before, when he traveled his way. Tom soon realized that he was being taken out of there.

Chapter 26

The Faction

Tom opened his eyes to find himself in yet another laboratory. This one was large and round, with a man waiting for him there.

"Hello Tom, my name is Todd Deckard. I'm sure you have heard of me at this point."

"I know who you are. Why did you bring me here?" Tom asked.

"You're the main character."

"What do you mean?"

"You've played the biggest part in this, even though you didn't know it. Theo over there," Tom looked over to see the man in glasses who had been a scientist at Shadow Corporation, the man waved with one hand, "was using the data gathered from the Shadow Corporation to put together this whole operation. It wasn't until we had the scans of your bioenergy that everything finally fell into place. Your energy is a bit different than most people, it is stronger. You were born with it free and as a result, it grew exponentially throughout your life. Most people only have a small stream of connection with it because they are taught by society to block it. You will be our catalyst. Our group of researchers found a way to use the data we gathered from you to open up the connection in everyone. We are going to make the whole world like us."

"What's to stop me from leaving?"

"Ha. Nothing, but we don't actually need you here with us to complete our plans. As long as you are somewhere in the universe, we will be able to connect with you and use the genetic details to activate Project Alpha. Think of the alternative. We could keep bombing buildings in an effort to persuade the people. Somehow I think you want to protect people, if you're anything like Jack and the others in your group. They are more worried about a few lives now than the future."

"You mean the future where you turn everyone into us?" Tom asked.

"That's the one. I was going about it all wrong trying to rid the world of normal people violently. It is much easier and more effective to do it this way. The fact is, everyone has the potential to be one of us, it is an inherent trait in all of us. The biggest thing keeping us from being alike is a genetic and mental block. We are going to use you to take away the genetic block. Everyone will have the power you do, and then nobody will be around to persecute people who don't have powers. It will eschew in an era of world peace and scientific advancement."

"What about the people who don't want this? It should be their choice. It is the source of a lot of suffering, even for me at times. The people who aren't ready for it won't be able to deal with it."

"An acceptable loss. We have calculated it as under 17% of the population that will suffer or die during the process of awakening."

"No loss is an acceptable one. Through the Shadow Corporation, we will find a way to integrate peacefully. In fact, we were already doing a good job of it," Tom said.

"No. You weren't. You were all hiding. Not letting the world see who you really were for fear of how they would react. Hiding isn't integrating."

"If we all reacted the way you are right now, then they should be afraid of us. You are no better than they are."

"No. Don't compare me to them. They had their chance to accept us. We could have all lived peacefully, but they were too scared of what we could do. They killed an innocent child, in cold blood, and now they get to see what it is like to have the same power. I thought you would approve, Tom. This is as peaceful as it can be. Hardly anybody will have to go through hate and anger. It will all happen at once, minimal suffering, in the blink of an eye. No one will have to kill anyone else. We are taking the responsibility in our own hands to create world peace!"

"What makes you think I won't stop you?"

"Tom. Quite the contrary, I thought you would be happy for us. I thought you would want to join us. When the world is rebuilt on special individuals, I want you to be on top with us."

"I could kill all of you right now, in the blink of an eye," Tom said, immediately regretting his decision to turn to petty threats.

"I think you already would have if you were capable. You're not a murderer, and even if you were, you know how the universe works. Everything happens as it must. You have no way of killing me before my time."

"I could go back and stop myself from being born. Then you would have nobody to use for your plan."

"I know you're not a murderer. That might even be suicide, but you know that it can't be done. Your life has already been put in place, it is the way things were written. You can't change things that massive, just as you won't be able to change this."

As he was saying this, two figures appeared in the room. One was an older man with crazy white hair in a lab-coat and the other an androgynous young man who had his legs crossed in lotus position and his eyes closed.

"Everything is in motion. Some stories have already been written, while others are not yet decided," said the man in the labcoat.

"Is that Einstein?" Deckard asked with a look of surprise. It was Einstein.

"You can see him?" Tom asked.

"Yes. He can't be real, Einstein died a long time ago."

"It is my mental projection of them. My subconscious brings them up at times when I have questions that I can't answer alone."

"That is extraordinary. See, this is why we chose you! You have so much more power and control than anyone else. You could be a great leader! Help us usher in this new era!" said Deckard.

"That is not something I ever wanted."

"Who is the other guy?"

"That is Siddhartha, Guatam the Buddha. He is here to give us all a message."

Siddhartha held up one finger and then spoke to them, "Those who are under the delusion of the forces of nature bind themselves to the work of these forces. Let not the wise man who sees disturb the unwise who see not."

"Did he really say that?" Deckard asked.

"I don't know. Everything I have read or listened to puts itself into form in this way. It is subconsciously transferred to these images of knowledge and wisdom."

"I understand what they are trying to say, but I know what I'm doing. I have seen the future and the past. This is not a point you can change. Even if you did kill me, it wouldn't change anything. The process was activated before we even brought you here. It is already over. When the timer counts down in five minutes, everything will be the way we have always dreamed."

"No Deckard, that is only *your* dream. I can't let this happen. It is not up to us to force our beliefs on other people. If they agree or not, that is their choice. I understand that there are accidents and cruel things happen to both sides, but it is not the majority. It is a few select people who choose to deal with their feelings the wrong way. It's not fair to the majority to use the actions of the minority as an example."

"Tell that to Theo. It was his brother they kidnapped and killed. What if it had been you or your sister? Do you think your father would have acted any differently than I did? It would be him standing here doing the same thing. This had to happen. Everyone knew it would come down to a choice one day, them or us. I really wanted you to support me in this. Changing them to our side is a far more compassionate act than what we have been doing."

"You bombed Shadow Corporation and killed your own people!"

"They were people like me, but they are not my people anymore. Not since they chose their side and left me on mine. Besides, I warned Jack, and you were there to save almost everyone. I didn't do it to hurt them, it was supposed to get the public's attention to what has been going on. If they found out that our people were being persecuted, they might stand up for us and support our actions. Instead they covered it up."

"What if they told it how it was? People like us, attacking other people like us. That would have made all of our kind look bad."

"That wouldn't have happened."

"You can't know what would have happened, or you would have seen this already," Tom argued.

"It was the right choice to make. It gave us reason to retaliate. Even now, when we change everyone, it is going to look aggressive. People won't see the resolution we are coming to until we have reached the conclusion. If they had reported it accurately, things would have been different. We would have been standing our ground and asserting ourselves by doing this in memory of the people we lost, but instead we are going to be seen as... I don't know what. Time will tell. It doesn't matter. All that matters is the new world. By the looks of that timer, it is almost here," said Deckard.

Tom watched as the timer counted down the last five seconds. Nothing happened. It hit zero. He stood there waiting. There was a whirring sound that started slow and sped up, filling the whole area with the humming noise. The hairs on their arms stood up.

"I think it is time we leave," said Einstein, taking Buddha's hand and disappearing from the room.

Moving through this space felt like moving through water. The energy was being concentrated and gathered into the space around Tom. He could feel every little part of his being and the field around him. Tom could see his electrical field being interacted with. There were tiny blue lightning strikes at the edges of his field that were breaking in toward him. Tom could feel the new energy flowing through him competing with his old energy, interacting, making him stronger. He felt himself throughout the whole universe. Every person, every tree, every rock, all of it. Tom was everywhere at once, and it was all perfect. Peaceful. Quiet. Tom's whole body was glowing.

"Is this going to kill him?" Deckard asked.

"I don't know," said Theo, "the new age will come at some cost."

"It already has."

Tom's body started to disintegrate, slowly spreading the energy in a giant wave over the entire world. Everything would be changed in a matter of moments.

"Did it work?" asked Deckard.

"I don't know," said Theo, "we have to wait and see. Everything here shows that it was a success."

Back at the training facility, they had noticed Tom's disappearance. When Jack finished speaking, he gathered the group of them together: Sarah, Adam, Sam, and Special Agent Hamilton who had been called in to help.

"How long do we have before they attack?" Hamilton asked.

"I don't know," said Jack, "it could be any minute."

"Where did Tom go?" Sam asked. None of them had an answer for that until they started to feel the hair on their necks standing up. They could sense what was coming because of their abilities, and then it happened. The room was light blue for a moment as a wave of energy passed over everyone.

"I have felt that before," said Sam, "I feel it when I am around Tom."

"It is his energy," said Jack.

"What does it mean?" They could feel their bodies being charged, the energy was being distributed throughout the world, activating everything in them.

"Can anyone else feel this?" asked Sarah. She put her hands to her side and floated gently off the ground.

"Our powers have been completely unlocked," said Jack, "everyone's have."

"But what happened to Tom?" Sam asked, still wondering about her love over anything else.

"I am trying to sense where he is," said Jack, "but his energy is everywhere. There is no individual to lock on to, it is all one. Everything. Everyone."

"What could have done this?" asked Sarah.

"Deckard. This was his master plan. Not to respond in kind, but to wake everyone. He wanted everyone to understand what it was like to be one of us. He made it happen," Jack explained.

"You mean everyone has powers now?" Sam asked.

"They always did. There was just something stopping them. I don't feel it anymore. The blockage is cleared. Everything is flowing naturally," said Jack.

Chapter 27

Transformation

All over the world things were changing. People were changing. They were opening. It was like being let out of solitary confinement after a lifetime of aloneness. Getting out of a prison no one knew they were in. Everything was bright and beautiful. Overwhelmingly so. Some couldn't handle it and broke down like Tom had, or worse. They lost the most people in the first hour. There were those who just couldn't handle it. Everything was too much for them. They had been creating their own blocks for so long that they could not deal with reality anymore. What they believed, had become their reality, and nothing could replace it. Not even freedom.

Chaos. No one would ever want to work again. Nothing would ever be work again. It could all be done in the blink of an eye. Businesses would collapse, nobody wanted anything anymore or needed anything anymore. They could create anything their mind thought about. At first crime ran rampant as people tried to commit crimes all over the world, but the shop owners quickly repaired everything to the way it was, people couldn't die anymore except in rare cases when they would die with no known cause. It was the universe keeping everything on its timeline. Even though the humans were doing whatever they wanted with everything, the universe still kept track of what needed to happen. It made sure people died when they were supposed to and were born when they were supposed to. Everything would be different from then on. It was like a dream, as if the entire population had taken a drug, and it had finally worn off.

People flew through the air and appeared out of nowhere. They soon understood that there was nothing they could ever want. With the world at their fingertips, everything had become... boring. They had nothing to strive for, to work for. Nowhere to go. The ones who already had some idea of it, enjoyed existing in general and loved it, while others fought and rejected it. They had liked being slaves. There had to be more to life. Some of those people who had been freed were clinging on to everything. They had to have a purpose, a reason for existing. Groups were started of people who refused to use their powers. They would go to meetings and churches, talking about how it was impacting their lives. Some speculated the end of the world, while others, the beginning.

The world had been set free. Money became worthless. Nothing at all had meaning. It was all the same thing. Everyone, everything, all one. Tom had created the possibility of everyone being united, but there were still minds out there. Minds that rejected it, minds that wanted control. They still believed there was such a thing. People wanted money, women, power, control over others, all things they could no longer have or that they could easily have at a whim. No satisfaction or gratification in what they did. They didn't have meaning anymore. No value. Nothing did. People still talked to each other. It was the only way they could create separation, but they would know what the other person was going to say before it was said, and what they would say in return. Knowing the future was a blessing and a curse. Nothing could happen that wasn't already known and seen. It lacked surprise.

Deckard and his faction basked in the glory they had created. Knowing he had made the difference, Deckard inflated his sense of self. Until he realized that there was nowhere to go from here. He had planned on being a leader and running things, but there was no need for it anymore. No one needed leading. They all knew the secrets of the universe. They didn't need any one person to tell them what to do or what it meant. The knowledge was already there for everyone. It was a paradise but a new prison as well. There was freedom for all, except the freedom they had before this. The freedom to suffer. There was nothing that could cause suffering. The egoic mind was running rampant trying to think of things it could do to gain control. People were letting go and the mind couldn't handle it on this large of a scale. So many struggled for things that they couldn't have. It was a world of peace, but a world of confusion. So many people didn't know what to do. They had nothing to do. Some kept doing what they had always done as if nothing had changed, but it was only a small group of people. They would go to the office where no one else showed up and continue to do their job. It was such a lonely existence even though everyone was together. Together, yet separate. All one, but alone.

"We have to change it back," said Deckard, after a few months, "this isn't what it was supposed to be like. I see that now. There has to be two sides. It can't all be the same like this."

"I don't know if we can change it back. I wouldn't even know where to begin," said Theo.

"But we know everything, we are connected. We have to reverse it. How was it done when existence started? Isn't there a way to pull his energy back in to one place?"

195

"I'm afraid not. We do know everything. His energy has already dispersed to everything in the universe. If we pulled it all together it would destroy the very fabric of the universe. We both know that it's already been done and cannot be undone," said Theo.

"This is the price of peace. Listlessness. This feeling of loss, a negative emptiness, even though there was nothing there in the first place, it feels empty instead of full. We didn't know it would be this way," Deckard explained.

"There is only one man who can save us now... if that is what he wants," said Theo.

"Tom," said Deckard

"Tom," Theo agreed.

"Wherever he may have gone... God help him."

Chapter 28
Tom's Landing

The wind blew fiercely that day. There was a blue tint for the slightest moment as Tom appeared on the street. Everything seemed like it was okay. Maybe whatever they did to him had no effect.

"Boy, the mountains sure look angry today," said a man who was making small talk with Tom, "as I was coming in to town I could barely even see them in the distance because of all the dust this wind is bringing up."

They shielded themselves from the wind as it blew leaves and debris in their faces. The man continued walking to wherever it was he was headed. The wind stopped just long enough for Tom to realize where he was. He was in the past. The universe must have sent him here to fix what had happened. To change it. To prevent it. Knowing that everything he did might have an impact, he had to go to the only safe place he knew in this time, his own home. He blinked his eyes and opened them at home, but it was a different home than he had expected. It was his apartment with Sam. He went into the bedroom to think over where he was, and what he should do. Then Tom walked in the door, the other Tom. Past Tom.

"What are you doing here?" Past Tom demanded, "You know you're not supposed to mess with the timelines."

"I do know," said Future Tom, "the universe sent me. Something awful has happened in my time and I was sent back here to stop it. The universe made this decision, not me."

"What if someone see's you? You can't just walk around looking like me. It could change things. You need to disguise yourself so that you won't cause any adverse effects on the time line."

"Alright," said Future Tom. He changed form and became a good looking girl that felt familiar to him, even though he didn't recognize the image. He must have seen her in passing. "We have to be careful with the timelines," said Future Tom, "I'm sure whatever I have to do is going to change things for the better, but once I have done it, there will be no me in this world to make the same trip. I need you to come back to this time period at this date so that we will not create a redundancy. When the problem is fixed, there will be no need to come back, but if you don't come back it won't be fixed. See what I mean?"

"I understand, we have to prevent a paradox. That is why we don't mess with the timelines. Are you sure you're really me?"

"What? Of course I am. Who else would I be?"

"I don't know. It's just that your energy feels different somehow. I don't know what it means. You have a different connection to it. The moment you came here, I could see that it was to stop a young boy from being killed, but you don't seem to see even that much," said Past Tom.

"That is because you are unattached. You are not involved with this. As you get older, things will start to become important for reasons that I can't tell you right now," said Future Tom.

"How dreadful or... extraordinary! We just have to save the boy and then you can go back to your time and we will continue on like none of this happened," said Past Tom.

They heard someone come into the apartment and Tom realized what he had just done.

"Oh no, I can't believe this is my fault. I am sorry for this. I remember where I saw this face. Take off your shirt and open the bedroom door," said Future Tom.

Past Tom listened to Future Tom who was now in the guise of a woman. He didn't understand what was happening, because in his universe it wasn't going to happen. Future Tom had become the woman that Tom was about to be caught cheating with. He had cheated on her though, hadn't he? The memory was there. Had it been himself all along? Things were not straight. He was about to find out why. After Sam left upset, Past Tom gave Future Tom a dirty look and said, "That is why you don't mess with the timelines! Now we both look like terrible people. I would never cheat on Sam. Whatever you are preventing better be important enough to make up for this."

"It is," said Future Tom, "the whole world is at stake."

"Well, you may have just ruined my whole world. Wasn't there a better way to deal with that situation? One where I didn't look like the bad guy?"

"It's my world too. I have already lived with the repercussions, but don't worry, when you become me..."

"Stop. I don't need to know. The future needs to stay in the future."

"Will you help me find the boy?"

"I don't even want to know why you have so little control over your abilities. Everything is so easy for me, why is it so difficult for you? What could have made an attachment like that?"

"I guess I never thought about what it was like when I was younger. Everything is different for me. The world is different. I know I shouldn't say very much, but Sam is still important to me."

"I have already seen and heard too much from you. I'll probably have to have my memory erased after this so that it won't impact my future. I will have to write something over this, and in it I will have cheated on Sam. Why are you staring at me like that?" asked Past Tom.

"No reason. Things make so much more sense now. Can you help me save the boy?"

"Let's get it over with so I don't have anything else to fix because of you."

Future Tom was taken by Past Tom to an empty street where the boy was. The boy was skipping, floating for a step or two in between landing. He did have a connection. A van pulled up beside him and three men jumped out, surrounding him. This was the boy. They were going to take him and kill him. Tom had forgotten how easy it had been for him to do everything. The entire world was at his fingertips and he didn't do very much with it. He would have to work on building his connection and letting go of his attachments when he got back.

The two Tom's phased over to the boy, Future Tom still looking like the girl.

"Looks like we have more irregulars to deal with boys," said the leader of the group. He pulled out a knife and the three men stood their ground, "you are going to regret the day you messed with Wild Bill."

The boy was crying, not knowing what was going to happen to him.

"Oh, please," said Past Tom. He held up his hand and three of them grabbed at their throats gasping for air. "This is what you get, when you pick on little boys. You are old enough to know better. The world will be a safer place without you and your hate."

The boy, though slightly traumatized from the situation, would be okay. He ran down the street, home to his family.

"This isn't how we deal with things," said Future Tom.

"What's wrong with it? You getting soft? The world is better without them." The men were turning blue.

"How is it any better of us to kill them than for them to kill the boy? What makes us any different? We are supposed to be the good guys."

"They aren't innocent. That is the difference. They chose to do these things, and they made the wrong choice," said Past Tom.

"We have the power to change them."

"To make them like us?"

"No. That never works. The power to change their minds. To show them the error of their ways."

"By force?"

"If it comes to that," Future Tom said reluctantly.

"Go back home, Tom. You've done your part." Past Tom waved his hand at Future Tom, who was sent flying through space and time, back to when he had left.

"Wait!" Tom said, as he landed back into his time. It felt like the same day he had left, but his energy wasn't everywhere. It had worked. The device hadn't been activated, or even created. Everything happened properly. Without the boy's death, Deckard was never pushed over the edge. He never started the faction and had no one to get revenge on.

Tom looked around. He was back in the room with the two way mirror that looked like a window. His room at the Shadow Corporation. He went down the hall to the main room where everybody was hanging around relaxing.

"Ah, Tom, you're finally awake," said a man greeting him as if they were old friends. It was Wild Bill. The leader of the group that was going to kill the boy. What was he doing here? Tom was relieved that his past self hadn't killed the man, but was still on guard.

"What's he doing here?" Tom said to Sarah, who was the closest one to them.

"Always a kidder," said Wild Bill, as he walked away. Tom supposed that Wild Bill wasn't so wild anymore.

"He is one of the founding members," said Sarah, "one of the top four. He is here all the time helping kids to embrace their powers. You know that. You're acting funny, did something happen to you?"

"Wild Bill helped form the Shadow Corporation?" Tom asked, "just to be sure, with who else?"

"Shadow Corporation? Ha! That sounds so mysterious. Are people really calling it that? It's the Global Peace Initiative, Tom. That's what it has always been. It was started by our father, Mike Hamilton, Todd Deckard, and Bill Higgins, after tensions were rising between people with abilities and people without. They banded together to make the world a safe and peaceful place for everybody to live in. You are in a strange mood today. Are you feeling all right?"

"I'm fine. Where is Sam?"

"She's in her room. I think she has been waiting for you. Why don't you go see her?"

Tom knocked on her door and she answered.

"Hey sweetie," Sam said. She gave him a kiss on the cheek and invited him in, "how are you this morning?"

"Not bad," said Tom, "but there are some things I need to talk to you about." He didn't hold the suspense for very long, realizing that it always sounded like something worse than it was. He told her all about what had happened. A world where everyone had powers. Going back in time and becoming the other woman. He had never cheated on her. It had come as a surprise to him too. He told her all about Past Tom, the adventure they shared, and how the world had been shaped differently because of it. Sam smiled and nodded, listening to the whole story. Tom would never know if she believed him or not. After all, it was quite farfetched that the whole world could be awakened by a combination of Tom's power and science. It wasn't important. Things were better. Advancements to the human energy field were coming regularly, with the research being done by the Global Peace Initiative. For the first time, Tom had a family. A family where he fit in. They had even brought Tom's mom in to help. She had spent half of her life raising the strongest one of them.

Tom and Sam spent the rest of their days in love. They really started using the time that they had. I haven't talked to Tom in some time, but the last I heard they were still continuing on, year after year, staying the same as everything around them changed. They were two of a kind. In love until the very end. We can only hope for such strength in the love that we feel for one another. The lesson was learned. The best way to get rid of your enemies is to make them your friends, and the best way to keep your friends is to be open with them. Take your time when you are in situations that are both pleasant and unpleasant so that you can know what is really going on before you act. The world is a very big place and the people in it can sometimes be small. Don't let your mind lead you down the wrong path.

Prologue

There is a hand shown knocking on someone's front door. It is opened by a young Sam and we see that the person who knocked is a girl with green hair.

"Do I know you?" Sam asked.

"Not in a formal sense. I am Mary Jane. I was sent here on behalf of Tom."

"Oh great, what does he want."

"He has done something stupid... well, who am I to say that? Tom had his memories erased so that he wouldn't have to remember hurting you. Take this letter. If he sees it, his memories will be returned."

"I'm finding this hard to believe."

"If you know Tom as well as we do, then I don't think that's the case."

"Maybe it's better that he doesn't remember... sometimes I wish I could forget."

"Every moment of our lives shapes who we are. Don't give that up at any price."

"Tell me. Wherever he is... is he happy?"

"He is working toward it, but he will never truly be happy without you."

"I wish that were true. We're going to find him, you know. He is dangerous."

"He may not be the same person you remember, when you meet him at the store."

"We'll see," Sam said.

Mary Jane walked away from the house and disappeared as Sam closed the door.

Afterword

It has been a pleasure for me to tell Tom's story. I am one of the few trustworthy people Tom knew would tell nothing but the truth. I have not tried to make him or anyone else appear to be better or worse than the events and thoughts that occurred.

Who am I exactly? I am Tom and I am Sam. I am Adam. I am Jack. I am Sarah and I am Agent Hamilton. I am John and Mary Jane. I am you and I am me. I am everybody and I am nobody. We are all part of one another. I am existence. I am Buddha. I am the energy that permeates everything in the universe. I am the universe. I am the I but I am not. I am everything and I am nothing. I am the author but I did no writing. I am the observer, the reporter, and the player.

I will continue to tell stories of the great men that history forgot. I can only hope that others will learn from their example. The good. The bad. The mistakes they made, so that we will not have to. I have been as objective as I can and I am glad that you took the time to see what I had to show you. Tom's story may seem a bit out of the ordinary to most, but wait until the next story I have to tell before you make any judgement. This has only been a drop of water compared to the things I have seen. There is always more to come.

www.ingramcontent.com/pod-product-compliance
Lightning Source LLC
Chambersburg PA
CBHW051949220626
47052CB00004B/867